"You make me fe
long time. I'm so

He didn't wait for her
was going to listen to the word *can't* coming from
her, not when she'd basically told him she wanted
him. In one quick movement, he leaned down and
brushed his lips over hers.

The moment was cut short when a dog barked—the
sound coming from his house—and Emily pulled
back. "You have a dog?"

"A puppy," he said, scrubbing a hand over his jaw
and trying to get a handle on the lust raging through
him. "Ruby—my pup—was the runt. She was weaker
than the rest and her brothers and sister tended to
pick on her."

"You rescue puppies, too? Unbelievable."

"It's not a big deal."

"Tell that to Ruby." She reached up on tiptoe,
touched her lips to the corner of his mouth and
then moved away. "You're damn near perfect,
Jase Crenshaw."

"I'm not—"

"You are." She shook her head. "It's too bad for
both of us that I gave up on perfect."

* * *

CRIMSON, COLORADO:
Finding home—and forever—in the West

Dear Reader,

Did you ever daydream when you were younger about how your perfect life would look?

Emily Crawford had her future all planned out, and the one thing it didn't involve was returning to her hometown of Crimson, Colorado. But now she's back, a divorced single mother to a sweet boy with special needs. She's starting over and has no idea what her future holds, but she's determined to make a new life on her terms, if only someone will give her a chance.

Jase Crenshaw has been waiting for a chance with Emily, his best friend's sister, for as long as he can remember. But this Crimson native is as dedicated to the town as he is to repairing his family's reputation, and Emily's dreams of leaving Colorado far behind were one more thing that put her out of his reach.

But dreams change, and sometimes it takes an unexpected love to show two people that what they really need to make them happy has been right in front of them all along.

Thank you for returning to Crimson, Colorado, with me. I'd love to hear what you think of Emily and Jase's story. Drop me a line at michelle@michellemajor.com.

Happy reading!

Michelle

Always the Best Man

———

Michelle Major

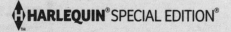
HARLEQUIN® SPECIAL EDITION®

Recycling programs
for this product may
not exist in your area.

ISBN-13: 978-0-373-65977-7

Always the Best Man

Copyright © 2016 by Michelle Major

All rights reserved. Except for use in any review, the reproduction or utilization of this work in whole or in part in any form by any electronic, mechanical or other means, now known or hereinafter invented, including xerography, photocopying and recording, or in any information storage or retrieval system, is forbidden without the written permission of the publisher, Harlequin Enterprises Limited, 225 Duncan Mill Road, Don Mills, Ontario M3B 3K9, Canada.

This is a work of fiction. Names, characters, places and incidents are either the product of the author's imagination or are used fictitiously, and any resemblance to actual persons, living or dead, business establishments, events or locales is entirely coincidental.

This edition published by arrangement with Harlequin Books S.A.

For questions and comments about the quality of this book, please contact us at CustomerService@Harlequin.com.

® and TM are trademarks of Harlequin Enterprises Limited or its corporate affiliates. Trademarks indicated with ® are registered in the United States Patent and Trademark Office, the Canadian Intellectual Property Office and in other countries.

Printed in U.S.A.

Michelle Major grew up in Ohio but dreamed of living in the mountains. Soon after graduating with a degree in journalism, she pointed her car west and settled in Colorado. Her life and house are filled with one great husband, two beautiful kids, a few furry pets and several well-behaved reptiles. She's grateful to have found her passion writing stories with happy endings. Michelle loves to hear from her readers at michellemajor.com.

Books by Michelle Major

Harlequin Special Edition

Crimson, Colorado

A Baby and a Betrothal
A Very Crimson Christmas
Suddenly a Father
A Second Chance on Crimson Ranch
A Kiss on Crimson Ranch

A Brevia Beginning
Her Accidental Engagement
Still the One

The Fortunes of Texas: All Fortune's Children

Fortune's Special Delivery

The Fortunes of Texas: Cowboy Country

The Taming of Delaney Fortune

Visit the Author Profile page
at Harlequin.com for more titles.

For Stephanie.
You have the strongest, bravest spirit of
any mother I know and you inspire me every day.

Chapter One

Some women were meant to be a bride. Emily Whitaker had been one of those women. For years she'd fantasized her walk down the aisle, imagining the lacy gown, the scent of her bouquet and the admiring eyes of family and friends as she entered the church.

When the day had finally arrived, there was no doubt she'd been beautiful, her shiny blond hair piled high on her head, perfect makeup and the dress—oh, her dress. She'd felt like a princess enveloped in so much tulle and lace, the sweetheart neckline both feminine and a little flirty.

Guests had whispered at her resemblance to Grace Kelly, and Emily had been foolish enough to believe that image was the same thing as reality. Her fairy tale had come true as her powerful white knight swooped her away from Crimson, the tiny Colorado mountain town where she'd grown up, to the sophisticated social circles of old-money Boston.

Too soon she discovered that a fantasy wedding was not the same thing as real marriage and a beautiful dress did not equate to a wonderful life. Emily lost her taste for both daydreams and weddings, so she wasn't sure how she'd found herself outside the swanky bridal boutique in downtown Aspen seven years after her own doomed vows.

"You can't want me as your maid of honor."

Katie Garrity, Emily's soon-to-be sister-in-law smiled. "Of course I do. I asked you, Em. I'd be honored to have you stand up with me." Katie's sweet smile faltered. "I mean, if you'll do it. I know it's short notice and there's a lot to coordinate in the next few weeks so…"

"It's not that I don't want to…"

Katie was as sweet as any of the cakes and cookies sold in the bakery she owned in downtown Crimson. She'd been a steadfast best friend to Emily's brother, Noah Crawford, for years before Noah realized that his perfect match had been right in front of him all along.

Emily was happy for the two of them, really she was. But if Katie was pure sugar, Emily was saccharine. She knew she was pretty to look at but after that first bite there was an artificial sweetness that left a cloying taste on the tongue. Emily didn't want her own bitterness to corrupt Katie's happy day.

"You have a lot of girlfriends. Surely there's a better candidate than me?"

"None of them are going to be my sister-in-law." Katie pressed her fingers to the glass of the shop's display window. "I remember the photos of your wedding that ran in *Town & Country* magazine. Noah and I don't want anything fancy, but I'd like our wedding to be beautiful."

"It will be more than beautiful." Emily swallowed back the anger that now accompanied thoughts of her marriage. "You two love each other, for better or worse." She took a breath as her throat clogged with emotion she'd thought had been stripped away during her divorce. She waved her hand in front of her face and made her voice light. "Plus all the other promises you'll make in the vows. But I'm not—"

"I'm a pregnant bride," Katie said suddenly, resting a hand on her still-flat stomach. She smiled but her eyes were shining. "I love your brother, Emily, and I know we'll have a good life together. But this isn't the order I planned things to happen, you know?"

"You and Noah were meant to be," Emily assured her. "Everyone knows that."

"Crimson is a small town with a long memory. People also know that I've had a crush on him for years and until I got pregnant, he had no interest in me."

Emily shook her head. "That's not how it happened." It had taken Katie walking away for Noah to realize how much she meant to him, but Emily knew his love for his fiancée was deep and true.

"It doesn't stop the talk. If I hear one more person whisper *shotgun wedding*—"

"Who?" Emily demanded. "Give me names and I'll take care of them for you." Since Emily had returned to Colorado at the beginning of the summer, she'd spent most of her time tucked away at her mother's farm outside town. She needed a do-over on her life, yet it was easier to hide out and lick her emotional wounds. But it wouldn't be difficult to ferret out the town's biggest gossips and grown-up mean girls. After all, Emily had been their ringleader once upon a time.

"What I need is for you to help me take care of the wedding," Katie answered softly. "To stand by my side and support me as I deal with the details. You may not care about the people in Crimson anymore, but I do. I want my big day to be perfect—as perfect as it can be under the circumstances. I don't want anyone to think I tried to force Noah or rush the wedding." She smoothed her fingers over her flowery shirt. "But I've only got a few weeks. Invitations have already gone out, and I haven't even started planning. Josh and Sara had one free weekend at Crimson Ranch this fall, and I couldn't wait any longer. I don't want to be waddling down the aisle."

"None of that matters to Noah. He'd marry you tomorrow or in the delivery room or whenever and wherever you say the word."

"It matters to me." Katie grimaced. "My parents are coming for the wedding. They haven't been to Crimson in years. I need it to be…" She broke off, bit down on her lip. "You're right. It doesn't matter. I love Noah, and I should just forget the rest of this. Why is a wedding such a big deal anyway?"

But Emily understood why, and she appreciated Katie's need for validation even if she didn't agree with it. So what if Emily no longer believed in marriage? She'd picked a husband for all the wrong reasons, but Katie and Noah were the real deal. If the perfect wedding would make Katie happy, then Emily would give her a day no one would forget.

"I could be the wedding planner, and you can ask one of your friends to—"

"I want *you*," Katie interrupted. "I'm an only child and now I'll have a sister. My family's messed up, but that makes me value the one I'm marrying into even more."

"I haven't valued them in the past few years." Emily felt her face redden, embarrassment over her behavior rushing through her, sharp and hot. "Until Davey was born I didn't realize how important family was to me."

"When your dad got sick, you helped every step of the way."

That much was true. Her father died when Emily was in high school. She'd taken over the care of the farm so her mom could devote time to Dad. Meg Crawford had driven him to appointments, cooked, cleaned and sat by his bedside in the last few weeks of home hospice care when the pancreatic cancer had ravaged his body.

It had been the last unselfish thing Emily had done in her life until she'd left her marriage, her so-called friends and the security of her life in Boston. As broken as she felt, she'd endure the pain and humiliation of those last six months again in a heartbeat for her son.

"You're a better person than you give yourself credit for," Katie said and opened the door of the store. The scent of roses drifted out, mingling with the crisp mountain air.

"I know exactly who I am." Emily removed her Prada sunglasses and tipped her face to the bright blue August sky. She'd missed the dry climate of Colorado during her time on the East Coast. It was refreshing to feel the warmth of the sun without miserable humidity making it feel like she'd stepped into an oven.

"Does that include being my maid of honor?" Katie asked over her shoulder, taking a step into the boutique.

"Shouldn't it be matron of honor?" Emily followed Katie, watching as she gingerly fingered the white gowns on the racks of the small shop. The saleswoman, an older lady with a pinched face, stepped forward. Emily waved her away for now. Shopping was one thing she could do with supreme confidence. Not much of a skill but today she'd put it to good use. "What's the protocol for having a divorcée as part of the bridal party?"

"I'm sticking with maid. There's nothing matronly about you." Katie pulled out a simple sheath dress, then frowned when Emily shook her head. "I think it's pretty."

"You have curves," Emily answered and pointed to Katie's full chest. "Especially with a baby on board. We want something that enhances them, not makes you look like a sausage."

Katie winced. "Don't sugarcoat it."

"We've got a couple of weeks to pull off the most amazing wedding Crimson has ever seen. You can be sweet. I don't have time to mess around."

"It doesn't have to be—"

Emily held up a hand, then stepped around Katie to pull a dress off the rack. "It's going to be. This is a good place to start."

Katie let out a soft gasp. "It's perfect. How did you do that?"

The dress was pale ivory, an empire waist chiffon gown with a lace overlay. It was classic but the tiny flowers stitched into the lace gave a hint of whimsy. The princess neckline would look beautiful against Katie's dark hair and creamy skin and the cut would be forgiving if she "popped" in the next few weeks. Emily smiled a little as she imagined Noah's reaction to seeing his bride for the first time.

"You're beautiful, Katie, and we're going to find the right dress." She motioned to the saleswoman. "We'll start with this one," she said, gently handing over the gown.

The woman nodded. "When is the big day?"

"Two weeks," Emily answered for Katie. "So we'll need something that doesn't have to be special ordered."

"Anything along this wall is in stock." The woman turned to Katie. "The fitting room is in the back. I'll hang the dress."

"Do I have to plan a cheesy bachelorette party, too?" Emily selected another dress and held it up for Katie's approval.

Katie ignored the dress, focusing her gaze on Emily. "Is that your way of saying you'll be my maid of honor?"

Emily swallowed and nodded. This was not a big deal, two weeks of support and planning. So why did she feel like Katie was doing her the favor by asking instead of the other way around? "If you're sure?"

"Thank you," Katie shouted and gave Emily a huge hug.

This was why, she realized, as tears pricked the backs of her eyes. Emily hadn't had a real friend in years. The women who were part of her social circle in Boston had quickly turned on her when her marriage imploded, making her an outcast in their community. She'd burned most of her bridges with her Colorado friends when she'd dropped out of college to follow her ex-husband as he started his law career. Other than her mom and Noah, she had no one in her life she could count on. Until now.

She shrugged out of Katie's grasp and drew in a calming breath. "Who else is in the bridal party?"

"We're not having any other attendants," Katie told her. "I'll try on this one, too." She scooped up the dress and took a step toward the back of the store. "Just you and Jase. He's Noah's best man."

Emily stifled a groan and muttered, "Great." Jase Crenshaw had been her brother's best friend for years so she should have expected he'd be part of the wedding. Still, Crimson's favorite son was the last person she wanted to spend time with. He was the exact opposite of Emily—warm, friendly, easy-to-like. Around him her skin itched, her stomach clenched and she was generally made more aware of her long list of shortcomings. A real prince among men.

Katie turned suddenly and hugged Emily again. "I feel so much better knowing you're with me on this. For the first time I believe my wedding is going to be perfect."

Emily took another breath and returned the hug. She could do this, even with Jase working alongside her. Katie and Noah deserved it. "Perfect is my specialty," she told her friend with confidence. Behind her back, she kept her fingers crossed.

"What the hell was that?" Noah Crawford held out a hand to Jason Crenshaw, who was sprawled across the Crimson High School football field, head pounding and ears ringing.

Jase hadn't seen the hit coming until he was flat on his back in the grass. He should have been paying more attention, but in the moment before the ball was snapped, Emily Whitaker appeared in the stands. Jase had done his best to ignore the tall, willowy blond with the sad eyes and acid tongue since she'd returned to town.

Easier said than done since she was his best friend's sister and…well, since he'd had a crush on her for as long as he could remember. Since the first time she'd come after Jase and Noah for ripping the head from her favorite Barbie.

Emily'd packed quite a wallop back in the day.

Just not as much as Aaron Thompson, the opposing team's player who'd sacked Jase before running the ball downfield. Jase brushed away Noah's outstretched hand and stood, rubbing his aching ribs as he did. "I thought this was flag football," he muttered as he turned to watch Aaron do an elaborate victory dance in the end zone.

"Looks like Thompson forgot," Noah said, pulling off his own flag belt, then Jase's as they walked toward the sidelines.

"We'll get 'em next time." Liam Donovan, another teammate and good friend, gave Jase's shoulder a friendly shove. "If our quarterback can stay on his feet."

"This is a preseason game anyway," Logan Travers added. "Doesn't count."

"It counts that we whipped your butts," Aaron yelled, sprinting back up the field. He launched the game ball at Jase's head before Logan stepped forward and caught it.

"Back off, Thompson," Logan said softly, but it was hard to miss the steel in his tone. Logan was as tall as Jase's own six feet three inches but had the muscled build befitting the construction work he did. Jase was in shape, he ran and rock climbed in his free time. He also spent hours in front of his computer and in the courtroom for his law practice, so he couldn't compete with Logan's bulk.

He also wasn't much for physical intimidation. Not that Aaron would be intimidated by Jase. The Thompson family held a long-standing grudge against the Crenshaws, and hotheaded Aaron hadn't missed a chance to poke at him since they'd been in high school. Aaron's father, Charles, had been the town's sheriff back when Jase's dad was doing most of his hell raising and had made it clear he was waiting for Jase to carry on his family's reputation in Crimson.

Jase took a good measure of both pride and comfort in living in his hometown, but there were times he wished for some anonymity. They weren't kids anymore, and Jase had long ago given up his identity as the studious band geek who'd let bullies push him around to keep the peace.

He stepped forward, crossing his arms over his chest as he looked down his nose at the brutish deputy. "Talk is cheap, Aaron," he said. "And so are your potshots at me. We'll see you back on the field next month."

"Can't wait," Aaron said with a smirk Jase wanted to smack right off his face.

The feeling only intensified when Aaron jogged over to talk to Emily, who was standing with Katie and the other team wives and girlfriends on the sidelines.

"Let it go." Noah hung back as their friends approached the group of women. "She wouldn't give him the time of day in high school, and now is no different."

"Nice," Jase mumbled under his breath. "Aaron and I actually have something in common."

Noah laughed. "Katie's asked Emily to be the maid of honor. You'll have plenty of excuses to moon over her in the next few weeks."

Jase stiffened. "I *don't* moon."

"You keep telling yourself that," Noah said as he gave him a shove. "It doesn't matter anyway. Emily has her hands too full with Davey and starting over even if she wanted a man." He gave Jase a pointed, big-brother look. "Which she doesn't."

"I'm no threat," Jase said, holding up his hands. "Nothing has changed from when we were twelve. Your sister can't stand me."

"I get that but you'll both have to make an effort for the wedding. Katie doesn't need any extra stress right now."

"Got it," Jase agreed and glanced at his watch. "I've got to check in at the office before I head home."

"How's the campaign going?"

"Not much to report. It seems anticlimactic to run for mayor unopposed. Not much work to do except getting out the vote."

"You're more qualified for the position than anyone else in Crimson," Noah told him, "although I'm still not sure why city council and all the other volunteer work you do isn't enough?"

"I love this town, and I think I can help it move forward."

Noah smiled. "Emily calls you Saint Jase."

Jase felt his jaw tighten. "How flattering."

"She might have a point. What are your plans for the weekend? Katie and I are going out to Mom's place for a barbecue tomorrow night. Want to join us?"

Jase rarely had plans for the weekend. Juggling both

his law practice and taking care of his dad left little free time. But Emily would be there and while the rational part of him knew he shouldn't go out of his way to see her, the rest of him didn't seem to care. If he could get his father settled early tomorrow…

"Sounds good. What can I bring?"

"Really?" Noah's brows lifted. "You're venturing out on a Saturday night? Big time. We've got it covered. Come out around six."

"See you tomorrow," he said and headed over to his gym bag at the far side of the stands. He stripped off his sweaty T-shirt and pulled a clean one from the bag. As he straightened, Emily walked around the side of the metal bleachers, eyes glued to her cell phone screen as her thumbs tapped away. He didn't have time to voice a warning before she bumped into him.

As the tip of her nose brushed his bare chest, she yelped and stumbled back. The inadvertent touch lasted seconds but it reverberated through every inch of his body.

His heart lurched as he breathed her in—a mix of expensive perfume and citrus-scented shampoo. Delicate and tangy, the perfect combination for Emily. Noah had accused him of mooning but what he felt was more. He wanted her with an intensity that shook him to his core after all these years.

He'd thought he had his feelings for Emily under control, but this was emotional chaos. He was smart enough to understand it was dangerous as hell to the plans he had for his future. At this moment he'd give up every last thing to pull her close.

Instead he ignored the instinct to reach for her. When she was steady on her feet, he stepped away, clenching his T-shirt in his fists so hard his fingers went numb. "Looks like texting and walking might be as ill-advised as texting and driving."

"Thanks for the tip," she snapped, tucking her phone into the purse slung over her shoulder. Was it his imagination or was she flushed? Her breathing seemed as irregular as his felt. Then her pale blue eyes met his, cool and impassive. Of course he'd imagined Emily having any reaction to him beyond distaste. "My mom sent a photo of Davey."

"Building something?" he guessed.

"How do you know?"

"I was at the hospital the day of your mom's surgery. I made Lego sets with him while everyone was in the waiting room."

She gave the barest nod. Emily's mother, Meg, had been diagnosed with a meningioma, a type of brain tumor, at the beginning of the summer, prompting both Emily and Noah to return to Crimson to care for her. Luckily, the tumor had been benign and Meg was back to her normal, energetic self.

The Crawford family had already endured enough with the death of Emily and Noah's father over a decade ago. Having been raised by a single dad who was drunk more often than he was sober, Jase had spent many afternoons, weekends and dinners with the Crawfords. Meg was the mother he wished he'd had. Hell, he would have settled for an aunt or family friend who had a quarter of her loving nature.

But she'd been it, and lucky for Jase, Noah had been happy to share his mom and her affection. With neither of her kids living in town until recently and Meg never remarrying, Jase had become the stand-in when she had a leaky faucet that needed fixing or simply wanted company out at the family farm. He'd taken the news of her illness almost as hard as her real son.

"I remember," she whispered, not meeting his gaze.

"Every time I've been out to the farm this summer, Davey was building something. Your boy loves his Lego sets. He's—"

"Don't say obsessed," she interrupted, eyes flashing.

"I was going to say he has a great future as an engineer."

"Oh, right." She crossed her arms over her chest, her gaze dropping to the ground.

"I know five is young to commit to a profession," he added with a smile, "but Davey is pretty amazing." Something in her posture, a vulnerability he wouldn't normally associate with Emily made him add, "You're doing a great job with him."

Her rosy lips pressed together as a shudder passed through her. He'd meant the compliment and couldn't understand her reaction to his words. But she'd been different since her return to Crimson—fragile in a way she never was when they were younger.

"Emily." He touched a finger to the delicate bone of her wrist, the lightest touch but her gaze slammed into his. The emotion swirling through her eyes made him suck in a breath. "I mean it," he said, shifting so his body blocked her from view of the group of people still standing a few feet away on the sidelines. "You're a good mom."

She stared at him a moment longer, as if searching for the truth in his words. "Thanks," she whispered finally and blinked, breaking the connection between them. He should step away again, give her space to collect herself, but he didn't. He couldn't.

She did instead, backing up a few steps and tucking a lock of her thick, pale blond hair behind one ear. Her gaze dropped from his, roamed his body in a way that made him warm all over again. Finally she looked past him to their friends. "Katie told me you're the best man."

He nodded.

"I've got some ideas for the wedding weekend. I want it to be special for both of them."

"Let me know what you need from me. Happy to help in any way."

"I will." She straightened her shoulders and when she looked at him again, it was pure Emily. A mix of condescension and ice. "A good place to start would be putting on some clothes," she said, pointing to the shirt still balled in his fist. "No one needs a prolonged view of your bony bod."

It was meant as an insult and a reminder of their history. She'd nicknamed him Bones when he'd grown almost a foot the year of seventh grade. No matter what he'd eaten, he couldn't keep up with his height and had been a beanpole, all awkward adolescent arms and legs. From what he remembered, Emily hadn't experienced one ungainly moment in all of her teenage years. She'd always been perfect.

And out of his league.

He pulled the shirt over his head and grabbed his gym bag. "I'll remember that," he told her and walked past her off the field.

Chapter Two

Emily lifted the lip gloss to her mouth just as the doorbell to her mother's house rang Saturday night. She dropped the tube onto the dresser, chiding herself for making an effort with her appearance before a casual family dinner. Particularly silly when the guest was Jase Crenshaw, who meant nothing to her. Who probably didn't want to be in the same room with her.

Not when she'd been so rude to him after the football game with her reference to his body. He had to know the insult was absurd. He might have been a tall skinny teen but now he'd grown into his body in a way that made her feel weak in the knees.

That weakness accounted for her criticism. Emily had spent the last year of her marriage feeling fragile and unsettled. Jase made her feel flustered in a different way, but she couldn't allow herself be affected by any man when she was working so hard to be strong.

Of course she'd known Jase liked her when they were younger, but she hadn't been interested in her brother's best friend or anyone from small-town Crimson. Emily'd had her sights set on bigger things, like getting out of Colorado. Henry Whitaker and his powerful family had provided the perfect escape at the time.

Sometimes she wished she could ignore the changes in herself. She glanced at the mirror again. The basics were the same—blond hair flowing past her shoulders, blue eyes and symmetrical features. People would still look at her and see a beautiful woman, but she wondered if anyone saw beyond the surface.

Did they notice the shadows under her eyes, the result of months of restless nights when she woke and tiptoed to Davey's doorway to watch him sleeping? Could they tell she couldn't stop the corners of her lips from perpetually pulling down, as if the worry over her son was an actual weight tugging at their edges?

No. People saw what they wanted, like she'd wanted to see her ex-husband as the white knight that would sweep her off to the charmed life she craved. Only now did she realize perfection was a dangerous illusion.

She heard Jase's laughter drift upstairs and felt herself swaying toward the open door of the bedroom that had been hers since childhood. Her mom had taken the canopy off the four-poster bed and stripped the posters from the walls, but a fresh coat of paint and new linens couldn't change reality.

Emily was a twenty-eight year old woman reduced to crawling back to the financial and emotional safety of her mother's home. She dipped her head, her gaze catching on a tiny patch of pink nail polish staining the corner of the dresser. It must have been there for at least ten years, back when a bright coat of polish could lift her spirits. She'd had so many dreams growing up, but now all she wanted was to make things right for her son.

"Em, dinner is almost ready," her mom called from the bottom of the stairs.

"Be right there," she answered. She scraped her thumbnail against the polish, watching as it flaked and fell to the floor. Something about peeling a bit of her girlhood from the dresser made her breathe easier and she turned for the door. She took a step, then whirled back and picked up the lip gloss, dabbing a little on the center of her mouth and pressing her lips together. Maybe she couldn't erase the shadows under her eyes, but Emily wasn't totally defeated yet.

Before heading through the back of the house to the patio where Noah was grilling burgers, she turned at the bottom of the stairs toward her father's old study. Since she and Davey had returned, her mom had converted the wood-paneled room to building block headquarters. It had been strange, even ten years after her father's death, to see his beloved history books removed from the shelves to make room for the intricate building sets her son spent hours creating. Her mother had taken the change easier than Emily, having had years alone in the house to come to terms with her husband's death. That sense of peace still eluded Emily, but she liked to think her warmhearted, gregarious father would be happy that his office was now a safe place for Davey.

Tonight Davey wasn't alone on the thick Oriental rug in front of the desk. Jase sat on the floor next to her son, long legs sprawled in front of him. He looked younger than normal, carefree without the burden of taking care of the town weighing down his shoulders. Both of their heads were bent to study something Jase held, and Emily's breath caught as she noticed her son's hand resting on Jase's leg, their arms brushing as Davey leaned forward to hand Jase another Lego piece.

She must have made a sound because Jase glanced up, an almost apologetic smile flashing across his face. "You found us," he said and handed Davey the pieces before standing. Davey didn't look at her but turned toward his current model, carefully adding the new section to it.

"Dinner's ready," she said, swallowing to hide the emotion that threatened to spill over into her voice.

Jase had known her too long to be fooled. "Hope it's okay I'm in here with him." He gestured to the bookshelves that held neat rows of building sets. "He's got an impressive collection."

"He touched you," she whispered, taking a step back into the hall. Not that it mattered. Her son wasn't listening. When Davey was focused on finishing one of his creations, the house could fall down around him and he wouldn't notice.

"Is that bad?" Jase's thick brows drew down, and he ran a hand through his hair, as if it would help him understand her words. His dark hair was in need of a cut and his fingers tousled it, making her want to brush it off his forehead the way she did for Davey as he slept.

"It's not…it's remarkable. He was diagnosed with Asperger's this summer. It was early for a formal diagnosis, but I'd known something was different with him for a while." Emily couldn't help herself from reaching out to comb her fingers through the soft strands around Jase's temples. It was something to distract herself from the fresh pain she felt when talking about

Davey. "Building Lego sets relaxes him. He doesn't like to be touched and will only tolerate a hug from me sometimes. To see him touching you so casually, as if it were normal…"

Jase lifted his hand and took hold of hers, pulling it away from his head but not letting go. He cradled it in his palm, tracing his thumb along the tips of her fingers. She felt the subtle pressure reverberate through her body. Davey wasn't the only one uncomfortable being touched.

Since her son's symptoms had first started and her ex-husband's extreme reaction to them had launched the destruction of their family, Emily felt like she was made of glass.

Now as she watched Jase's tanned fingers gently squeeze hers, she wanted more. She wanted to step into this tall, strong, good man who could break through her son's walls without even realizing it and find some comfort for herself.

"I'm glad for it," he said softly, bringing her back to the present moment. "What about his dad?"

She snatched away her hand, closed her fist tight enough that her nails dug small half-moons into her palm. "My ex-husband wanted a son who could bond with him tossing a ball or sailing. The Whitakers are a competitive family, and even the grandkids are expected to demonstrate their athletic prowess. It's a point of pride and bragging rights for Henry and his brothers—whose kid can hit a ball off the tee the farthest or catch a long pass, even if it's with a Nerf football."

Jase glanced back at her son. "Davey's five, right? It seems a little young to be concerned whether or not he's athletic."

"That didn't matter to my in-laws, and it drove Henry crazy. He couldn't understand it. As Davey's symptoms became more pronounced, his father pushed him harder to be the *right* kind of boy."

She pressed her mouth into a thin line to keep from screaming the next words. "He forbade me from taking him to the doctor to be tested. His solution was to punish him, take away the toys he liked and force him into activities that ended up making us all more stressed. Davey started having tantrums and fits, which only infuriated Henry. He was getting ready to run for congress." She rolled her eyes. "The first step in the illustrious political campaign his family has planned."

"Following in his father's footsteps," Jase murmured.

It was true. Emily had married into one of the most well-known political families in the country since the Kennedys. The Whitakers had produced at least one US senator in each of the past five generations of men, and one of Henry's great-uncles had been vice president. "I didn't just marry a man, I took on a legacy. The worst part was I went in with my eyes open. I practically interviewed for the job of political wife, and I was ready to be a good one." She snapped her fingers. "I could throw a party fit for the First Lady with an hour's notice."

Jase cleared his throat. "I'm sure your husband appreciated that."

She gave a harsh laugh. "He didn't appreciate it. He expected it. There's a big difference." She shrugged. "None of it mattered once Davey was born. I knew from the time he was a baby he was different and I tried to hide...tried to protect him from Henry as long as possible. But once I couldn't anymore, there was no doubt about my loyalty." She plastered a falsely bright smile on her face. "So here I am back in Crimson."

Davey looked up from his building set. "I'm finished, Mommy."

She stepped around Jase and sat on the carpet to admire the intricate structure Davey had created. "Tell me about it, sweetie."

"It's a landing pod with a rocket launcher. It's like the ones they have on *The Clone Wars*, only this one has an invisible force field around it so no one can destroy it."

If only she could put a force field around her son to protect him from the curiosity and potential ridicule that could come due to his differences from other kids. "I love it, Wavy-Davey."

One side of his mouth curved at the nickname before he glanced at Jase. "He helped. He's good at building. Better than Uncle Noah or Grammy."

"High praise," Jase said, moving toward the bookshelves. "If you make a bridge connecting it to this one, you'd have the start of an intergalactic space station."

Emily darted a glance at Davey as Jase moved one of the sets a few inches to make room for this new one. Her boy didn't like anyone else making decisions about the placement of his precious building sets. To her surprise, Davey only nodded. "I'll need to add a hospital and mechanic's workshop 'cause if there's a battle they'll need those."

"Maybe a cafeteria and bunk room?" Jase suggested.

"You can help me with those if you want." Leaving Emily speechless where she sat, Davey gently lifted the new addition and carried it to the bookshelf. With Jase's help, he slid it into place with a satisfied nod. "I'm hungry. Can we eat?" he asked, turning to Emily.

"Sure thing," she agreed. "Grammy, Uncle Noah and Aunt Katie are waiting." Her family was used to waiting as transitions were one of Davey's biggest challenges. Sometimes it took long minutes to disengage him from a project.

Her son stepped forward, his arms ramrod straight at his sides. "It's time, Mommy. I'm ready."

She almost laughed at the confusion clouding Jase's gaze. People went in front of a firing squad with more enthusiasm than Davey displayed right now. It would have been funny if this ritual didn't break her heart the tiniest bit. Embarrassment flooded through her at what Jase might think, but the reward was too high to worry about a little humiliation.

She rose to her knees and opened her arms. Davey stepped forward and she pulled him close, burying her nose in his neck to breathe him in as she gave him a gentle hug. A few moments were all he could handle before he squirmed in her embrace. "I love you," she whispered before letting him go.

He met her gaze. "I know," he answered simply, then turned and walked out of the room.

She stood, wiping her cheeks. Why bother to hide the tears? She'd left the lion's share of her pride, along with most of her other possessions, back in Boston.

"Sorry," she said to Jase, knowing her smile was watery at best. Emily might be considered beautiful, but she was an ugly crier. "It's a deal he and I have. Every time he finishes a set, I get a hug. A real one."

"Emily," he whispered.

"Don't say anything about it, please. I can't afford to lose it now. It's dinnertime, and I don't need to give my family one more reason to worry about me."

A muscle ticked in his jaw, but he nodded. "In case no one has said it lately," he said as she moved past, "your ex-husband may be political royalty, but he's also a royal ass. You deserve to be loved better." The deep timbre of his voice rumbled through her like a cool waterfall, both refreshing and fierce in its power.

She shivered but didn't stop walking out of the room. Reality kept her moving forward. Davey was her full reason for being now. There was no use considering what she did or didn't deserve.

Chapter Three

"Is that you, Jase?"

"Yeah, Dad." Jase slipped into the darkened trailer and flipped on the light. "I'm here. How's it going?"

"I could use a beer," Declan Crenshaw said with a raspy laugh. "Or a bottle of whiskey. Any chance you brought whiskey?"

His father was sprawled on the threadbare couch that had rested against the thin wall of the mobile home since Jase could remember. Nothing in the cramped space had changed from the time they'd first moved in. The trailer's main room was tiny, barely larger than the dorm room Jase had lived in his first year at the University of Denver. From the front door he could see back to the bedroom on one side and through the efficiency kitchen with its scratched Formica counters and grainy wood cabinets to the family room on the other.

"No alcohol." He was used to denying his dad's requests for liquor. Declan had been two years sober and Jase was hopeful this one was going to stick. He was doing everything in his power to make sure it did. Checking on his dad every night was just part of it. "How about water or a cup of tea?"

"Do I look like the queen of England?" Declan picked up the potato chip bag resting next to him on the couch and placed it on the scuffed coffee table, then brushed off his shirt, chip crumbs flying everywhere.

"No one's going to mistake you for royalty." Jase's dad looked like a man who'd lived a hard life, the vices that had consumed him for years made him appear decades older than his sixty years. If the alcohol and smoking weren't enough, Declan had spent most of his adult life working in the active mines around Crimson, first the Smuggler silver mine outside of Aspen and then later the basalt-gypsum mine high on Crimson Mountain.

Between the dust particles, the constant heavy lifting, operating jackhammers and other heavy equipment, the work took a physical toll on the men and women employed by the mines. Jase had tried to get his father to quit for years, but it was only after a heart attack three years ago that Declan had been forced to retire. Unfortunately, having so much time on his hands had led him to a six-month drunken binge that had almost killed him. Jase needed to believe he wasn't going to have to watch his father self-destruct ever again.

"Maybe they should since you're a royal pain in my butt," Declan growled.

"Good one, Dad." Jase didn't take offense. Insults were like terms of endearment to his father. "Why are you sitting here in the dark?" He picked up the chip bag and dropped it in the trash can in the kitchenette, then started washing the dishes piled in the sink.

"Damn cable is out again. I called but they can't get here until tomorrow. If I lose my DVRed shows, there's gonna be hell to pay. *The Real Housewives* finale was on tonight. I wanted to see some rich-lady hair pulling."

Jase smiled. Since his dad stopped drinking, he'd become addicted to reality TV. Dance moms, little people, bush people, swamp people, housewives. Declan watched them all. "Maybe you should get a hobby besides television. Take a walk or volunteer."

His dad let out a colorful string of curses. "My only other hobby involves walking into a bar, so I'm safer holed up out here. And I'm not spending my golden years working for free. Hell, I barely made enough to pay the bills with my regular job. There's only room for one do-gooder in this family, and that's you."

It was true. The Crenshaws had a long history of living on the wrong side of the law in Crimson. There was even a sepia-stained photo hanging in the courthouse that showed his great-great-grandfather sitting in the old town jail. Jase had consciously set out to change his family's reputation. Most of his life decisions had been influenced by wanting to be something different...something more than the Crenshaw legacy of troublemaking.

"I read in the paper that you're sponsoring a pancake breakfast next week."

Jase placed the last mug onto the dish drainer, then turned. "It's part of my campaign."

"Campaigning against yourself?" his dad asked with a chuckle.

"It's a chance for people to get to know me."

Declan stood, brushed off his shirt again. "Name one person who doesn't know you."

"They don't know me as a candidate. I want to hear what voters think about how the town is doing, ideas for the future—where Crimson is going to be in five or ten years."

His dad yawned. "Same place it's been for the last hundred years. Right here."

"You know what I mean."

"Yeah, I know." Declan patted Jase on the back. "You're a good boy, Jason Damien Crenshaw. Better than I deserve as a son. It's got to be killing Charles Thompson and his boys that a Crenshaw is going to be running this town." His dad let out a soft chuckle. "I may give ex–Sheriff Thompson a call and see what he thinks."

"Don't, Dad. Leave the history between us and the Thompsons in the past where it belongs." Jase didn't mention the hit Aaron had put on him during the football game, which would only make his father angry.

"You're too nice for your own good. Why don't you pick me up before the breakfast?" Declan had lost his license during his last fall from the wagon and hadn't bothered to get it reinstated. Jase took him to doctor's appointments, delivered groceries and ran errands—an inconvenience, but it also helped him keep track of Declan. Something that hadn't always been easy during the heaviest periods of drinking. "I'll campaign for you. Call it volunteer work and turn my image around in town."

Jase swallowed. He'd encouraged his father to volunteer almost as a joke, knowing Declan never would. But campaigning… Jase loved his dad but he'd done his best to distance himself from the reputation that followed his family like a plague. "We'll see, Dad. Thanks for the offer. Are you heading to bed?"

"Got nothing else to do with no channels working."

"I'll call the cable company in the morning and make sure you're on the schedule," Jase promised. "Lock up behind me, okay?"

"Who's going to rob me?" Declan swept an arm around the trailer's shabby interior. "I've got nothing worth stealing."

"Just lock up. Please."

When his father eventually nodded, Jase let himself out of the trailer and headed home. Although he'd driven the route between the trailer park and his historic bungalow on the edge of downtown countless times, he forced himself to stay focused.

Three miles down the county highway leading into town. Two blocks until a right turn onto his street. Four hundred yards before he saw his mailbox. Keeping his mind on the driving was less complicated than giving the thoughts and worries crowding his head room to breathe and grow.

He parked his silver Jeep in the driveway, since his dad's ancient truck was housed in the garage. It needed transmission work that Jase didn't have time for before it would run again, and Declan had no use for it without a license. But Jase couldn't bring himself to sell it. It represented something he couldn't name…a giving in to the permanence of caring for an aging parent that he wasn't ready to acknowledge.

He locked the Jeep and lifted his head to the clear night. The stars were out in full force, making familiar designs across the sky. He hadn't used his old telescope in years, but Jase never tired of stargazing.

Something caught his eye, and when he looked around the front of his truck everything in the world fell away except the woman standing in his front yard.

Emily.

He wasn't sure where she'd come from or how he hadn't noticed her when he pulled up. Out of the corner of his eye he saw her mom's 4Runner parked across the street.

She didn't say anything as he approached, only watched him, her hands clasped tight together in front of her waist. Her fingers were long and elegant like the rest of her. As much as he would never wish her pain, the fact that she wore no wedding ring made him perversely glad.

"Hi," he said when he was in front of her, then silently cursed himself. He was an attorney and a town council member, used to giving speeches and closing arguments to courtrooms and crowded meetings. The best he could come up with now was *Hi*? Lame.

"I owe you an apology," she whispered. "And I didn't want to wait. I hate waiting."

He remembered that about her and felt one side of his mouth curve. Her mother, Meg, had been an expert baker when they were kids and Emily had forever been burning her mouth on a too-hot cookie after school.

"You don't owe me anything."

She shook her head. "No, it's true. You were good with Davey tonight. Before bed he told me he wants to invite you for a playdate."

He chuckled. "I told you we bonded over plastic bricks."

"His father never bonded with him," she said with a

strangled sigh. "Despite my brother's best efforts, Noah has trouble engaging him." She shrugged, a helpless lift of her shoulders that made his heart ache. "Even I have trouble connecting with him sometimes. I understand it's the Asperger's, and I love him the way he is. But you're the first…friend he's ever had."

"He'll do fine at school."

"What if he doesn't? He's so special, but he's not like other boys his age."

"He's different in some ways, but kids manage through those things. I didn't have the greatest childhood or any real friends until I met your brother. I was too tall, too skinny and too poor. My dad was the town drunk and everyone knew it. But it made me stronger. I swear. Once I met Noah and your family took me in—"

"I didn't."

"No. You hated me being in your house."

"It wasn't about… I'm sorry, Jase. For how I treated you."

"Em, you don't have to—"

"I do." She stepped forward, so close that even in the pale streetlight he could see the brush of freckles across her nose. "I haven't been kind to you even since I've come back. It's like the nice part of my brain short-circuits when you're around."

"Good to know."

"What I said to you the other day on the football field about putting on your shirt."

He winced. "My bony bod…"

"Had nothing to do with it. You're not a skinny kid anymore. You must know…" She stopped, looked away, tugged her bottom lip between her teeth, then met his gaze again.

Something shifted between them; a current of aware-ness different than anything he'd experienced surged to life in the quiet night air.

"The women of this town would probably pay you to keep your shirt off." She jabbed one finger into his chest. "All. The. Time."

He laughed, because this was Emily trying to be nice and still she ended up poking him. "I'm popular at the annual car wash, but I figure it's because most of the other men on the council are so old no one wants them to have a heart attack while bending to soap up a front fender."

She didn't return his smile but eased the tiniest bit closer. "I didn't want you standing bare chested in front of me because I wanted to kiss you."

Jase sucked in a breath.

"I wanted to put my mouth on you, right there on the sidelines of the high school field with half of our friends watching." She said the words calmly, although he could see her chest rising and falling. He wasn't the only one having trouble breathing right now. "That's something different than when we were young. You make me feel things I haven't in a long time, and I don't know what to do about it. But it doesn't give me the right to be rude. I'm sorry, Jase. I can't—"

He didn't wait for her to finish. There was no way he was going to listen to the word *can't* coming from her, not when she'd basically told him she wanted him. In one quick movement, he leaned down and brushed his lips over hers.

So this was where she hid her softness, he thought. The taste of her, the feel of her mouth against his. All of it was so achingly sweet.

Then she opened her mouth to him and he deepened the kiss, threading his fingers through her hair as their tongues glided together. It was every perfect kiss he'd imagined and like nothing he'd experienced before. He wanted to stay linked with her forever, letting all of his responsibilities and the rest of the damn world melt away.

The moment was cut short when a dog barked—the sound coming from his house, and Emily pulled back. Her fingers lifted to her mouth and he wasn't sure whether it was to press his kiss closer or wipe it away. Right now it didn't matter.

"You have a dog?" she asked, glancing at his darkened front porch.

"A puppy," he said, scrubbing a hand over his jaw and trying to get a handle on the lust raging through him. "My former secretary Donna had a female Australian shepherd that got loose while in heat. They ended up with a litter of puppies, part shepherd and part who knows what?"

The barking turned into a keening howl, making him cringe. "Maybe elephant based on the size of their paws. But Ruby—my pup—was the runt. She was weaker than the rest and her brothers and sister tended to pick on her. They kept her, but it wasn't working with their other dogs. I went for dinner last week and…" The barking started again. "I need to let her out to do her business. Do you want to meet her?"

Emily shook her head and a foolish wave of disappointment surged through him.

"I need to get back to the farm. Mom thinks I was running to the store for…" She broke off, gave an embarrassed laugh, then looked at him again. "You rescue puppies, too? Unbelievable."

"It's not a big deal."

"Tell that to Ruby." She reached up on tiptoe, touched her lips to the corner of his mouth and then moved away. "You're damn near perfect, Jase Crenshaw."

"I'm not—"

"You are." She shook her head. "It's too bad for both of us that I gave up on perfect."

Before he could answer, she walked away. He waited, watching until she'd gotten in the SUV and pulled down his street. Until her taillights were swallowed in the darkness. Then the silence enveloped him once more, and he wondered if he'd dreamed the past few minutes.

An increasingly insistent bark snapped him back to the land of the wide-awake. He jogged to the front door and unlocked it, moving quickly to the crate in his family room. Her fluffy tail wagged and she greeted him with happy nips and yelps. He led her to the back door and she darted out, tumbling down the patio steps to find her perfect spot in-yard.

He sank down to the worn wood and waited for her to finish, lavishing praise when she wiggled her way back to him.

"I've got a story for you," he told the puppy as she covered him in dog slobber. "It's been quite a night, Ruby-girl."

Early Tuesday morning, Emily pasted a bright smile on her face before opening the door to Life Is Sweet, the bakery Katie owned in downtown Crimson. The soothing scent of sugar and warm dough washed over her as she automatically moved toward the large display case at the front of the shop.

The ambiance of the cozy bakery cheered her, even with the hellish morning of job interviews and application submissions she'd had. No surprise that businesses weren't lining up to hire an overqualified, single-mom college dropout who could only work part-time hours and needed to be able to take off when her son had a bad day. Yet it felt personal, as if the town she'd so easily left behind wasn't exactly opening its arms to welcome her back.

Life Is Sweet was different. With the warm yellow walls and wood beams stretching the length of the ceiling, the shop immediately welcomed customers both new and familiar. A grouping of café tables sat in one corner of the small space and the two women working the counter and coffee bar waved to her.

Katie pushed through the door to the back kitchen a moment later, carrying a large metal tray of croissants that she set on the counter.

"Should you be carrying pastries in your condition?" Emily asked with a laugh. Last weekend during dinner, Noah hadn't let Katie bring any of the serving bowls out to the table on the patio or clear the dishes. In fact, he'd all but insisted she sit the whole time they were at their mother's house. No matter what any of the women had told him about Katie and the baby remaining healthy despite normal activities, he couldn't seem to stop fawning over his wife-to-be.

Katie rolled her eyes. "I would have never guessed your brother had such an overprotective streak. He wants me to cut back even more on my hours at the bakery." She waved to one of the customers sitting at a café table, then looked at Emily. "I've hired a manager to run the front, but I'm still in charge of most of the baking. As long as my doctor says it's okay, I want to keep working."

"He'll get over it. I'll talk to him. Dad's death made him funny about keeping everyone he loves healthy." Her whole family had felt helpless when the pancreatic cancer claimed her father, and it had taken years for Noah to get over the guilt of not being around to help those last months.

When their mom had her health scare, Noah had returned to Crimson right away and remained at Meg's side for the duration of her recovery. But losing one parent and being scared for the other had taken a toll on him, and Emily understood his reasons for wanting Katie to be so careful.

"I know, and I love him for it." Katie sighed. "The morning sickness is done, so I feel great." She put all but two of the croissants in the case. "I'm just hungry all the time. Can I interest you in a coffee-and-croissant break? They're chocolate."

"How did you know I need chocolate?"

"Everyone needs chocolate." Katie set the remaining pastries on a plate, then poured Emily a cup of coffee and handed it to her. "You look like you've been through the job search gauntlet today." She got the attention of one of the women working the counter and mouthed "Five minutes." There was a line forming at the cash register so the worker gave her a harried nod. "Let's go to the kitchen. More privacy."

"You're swamped right now. I'm fine."

"Never too swamped for a snack," Katie answered and picked up the plate. She led Emily through a heavy swinging door into the commercial kitchen. "I'm going to sit on a stool while you take my picture and text it to Noah. You're the witness that I'm not working too hard."

Emily snapped the photo, sent it to her brother and then pulled off a piece of the flaky dough. "Fresh from the oven?" she asked as she popped the bite into her mouth. She climbed onto a stool next to Katie, trailing her fingers across the cool stainless steel counter.

"The best kind."

"If my brother becomes too much of a pain, I'll marry you," Emily said when she finished chewing. The croissant melted in her mouth, buttery and soft with the perfect amount of chocolate in the middle.

"Don't distract me with flattery," Katie answered but moaned as she took a bite. "What happened today?"

"No one feels a burning desire to hire the woman who publicly ridiculed the town on her way out."

Katie made a face. "It was a well-known fact that you had no plans to stay in Crimson any longer than necessary."

"Or maybe I got drunk one night and announced to a bar full of locals that I was too good to waste away in this…"

"*Hellhole mountain slum*, I think you called it."

"Right. Classy."

"And endearing," Katie agreed, clearly having trouble keeping a straight face.

"I'm stupid." Emily pressed her forehead to the smooth stainless steel, let it soothe the massive headache she could feel starting behind her eyes.

"You can make this better," Katie said, placing a hand on Emily's back. "Crimson has a long history of forgiving mistakes."

"And an even longer one of punishing people for them." She tipped her head to the side. "Look at how hard Jase has worked to make amends for trouble he didn't even cause."

"But people love him."

"Because he's perfect."

"Why are you so hard on him, Em?"

Emily shook her head, unable to put into words her odd and tumbling emotions around Jase.

"You could work for him," Katie said with a laugh.

"For Jase?" Emily asked, lifting her head. "What do you mean?"

"I'm joking," Katie said quickly. "From what I can tell it bothers you to be in the same room with him."

"That's not exactly true." Emily had really liked Jase kissing her. It had been easy to lose herself in the gentle pressure of his mouth. His hands cradling her face made her feel cherished. She'd wanted to plaster herself against him and forget she was alone, at least for a few minutes. She was definitely bothered by Jase, but not in the way Katie believed. "Is he hiring for his campaign?"

"No," Katie answered slowly, as if reluctant to share what she knew. "His secretary retired a few months ago."

"The one with the litter of puppies?"

"How did you know about that?"

Emily ignored the question. "Why hasn't he hired someone?"

"He won't say, but as far as I know he hasn't even interviewed anyone for the position." Katie took another bite of pastry. "There are plenty of people who would love to work with him."

"Plenty of single women," Emily clarified.

"He's pretty hot," Katie said, her smile returning. "Not as handsome as Noah, of course. He makes me—"

"I'm working on being a good friend." Emily held up a hand. "But I draw the line on listening to you ruminate on the hotness of my brother." She hopped off her stool and took a final drink of coffee. "Break's over, friend. I just got a tip on a job opening." She picked up the plate and walked it over to the sink.

"Are you sure that's a good idea?"

"Clearing my plate?"

"Asking Jase for a job."

Emily straightened her suit jacket and smiled, pretending the nervous butterflies zipping through her belly didn't exist. "I'm not sure, but when has that ever stopped me?"

She gave Katie a short hug. "Thanks for listening. You're a pro at this whole supportive girlfriend thing."

Katie returned her smile. "Good luck, Em."

"I've got this," Emily answered with more confidence than she felt. But bluffing was second nature to her, so she squared her shoulders and marched out of the bakery to get herself a job.

Chapter Four

Jase reached for the file folder on the far side of his desk just as he heard Emily call his name. His hand jerked, knocking over the cup of leftover coffee that sat on another stack of papers, dark liquid spilling across the messy top of his desk.

"Damn," he muttered, grabbing the old towel he'd stuffed under the credenza behind him. This wasn't the first time most of his work papers had been dyed coffee brown. The mug had been half-empty so this cleanup wasn't the worst he'd seen. He quickly wiped up the spill, then moved the wet files to the row of cabinets shoved along the far wall.

By the time he turned around, Emily stood inside the door to his office. Her blue gaze surveyed the disorder of his office before flicking back to him. "Is it always this bad?"

He kicked the dirty towel out of sight behind his

desk. "I've got things under control. It only looks like chaos."

She arched a brow. "Right."

Jase hadn't seen Emily since she'd walked away from him Saturday night. Letting her go had been one of the hardest things he'd ever done, but Emily wasn't the same proud, confident girl she'd been in high school. Whatever had happened when her marriage fell apart had left her bruised and tender. Jase had always been a patient man, and if she needed him to go slow he could force himself to honor that.

She didn't appear fragile now. This morning Emily wore a tailored skirt suit that looked like it cost more than the monthly rent on his office space. It was dark blue and the hem stopped just at her knee. Combined with low heels, a tight bun and a strand of pearls around her neck, Jase could imagine her on the stage next to her ex-husband, the perfect accessory for a successful politician.

He wanted to pull her hair loose, rip off the necklace that was more like a collar and kiss her until her skin glowed and her mouth turned pliant under his. Until he could make her believe she was more than the mask she wore like a coat of armor.

"Why haven't you hired a new secretary?"

He blinked, the question as much of a surprise as her appearance in his office. "I don't need one."

"Even you can't believe that." She nudged a precariously balanced pile of manila folders with one toe, then bent forward to right it when the stack threatened to topple.

"I haven't had time," he said, running a hand through his hair and finding it longer than he remembered. A haircut was also on his to-do list. "I did some inter-viewing when Donna first retired. She took a medical leave when her husband had a heart attack, and then they decided to simplify their lives and working here got cut. But she'd been with the practice when I took it over and ran this place and my life with no trouble at all. If I hire someone new, I'll have to train them and figure out if we can work together and…" He paused, not sure how to explain the rest.

"Let me guess." She arched a brow. "The women applying for the job think they're also interviewing for the role of your wife?"

"Maybe," he admitted, grabbing the empty coffee cup from his desk and walking toward her. There were plenty of single men in Crimson, so it was an irritat-ing mystery how he'd ended up on the top of the eli-gible bachelor list. He didn't have time for dating, and even if he did…

"It would have been easier if Donna had helped screen the applicants."

One side of her mouth curved even as she rolled her crystal-blue eyes. "Because you have trouble hurting their feelings."

"You think you've got me all figured out."

She shrugged. "You're nice, Jase. Not complicated."

He touched the tip of one finger to her strand of pearls. "Unlike you?"

She sucked in a breath and stepped back so he could pass. There was a small utility sink in the kitchenette off the hallway, and he added the cup to the growing pile of dirty dishes. When he turned around, Emily was standing behind him, holding four more mugs by their handles.

"You forgot these."

He sighed and reached for them. Add washing dishes to the list.

"I appreciate the social call, but was there a reason you stopped by?" He turned and moved closer, into her space. "Unless you want to continue what we started Saturday night. That kind of work break I can use."

"No break and Saturday night was a mistake." She frowned. "You and I both know it."

He wanted to kiss the tension right off her face. "Then why can't I stop thinking about how you felt pressed against me?" He dropped his voice. "The way you taste…"

Color rose to her cheeks.

"I'm not the only one, am I? You walked away but you came back." His fingers itched to touch her. "You're here now."

"This isn't a social call." Emily straightened the hem of her jacket, looking almost nervous. "I think you should hire me."

Jase almost laughed, then realized she was serious. "No." He shook his head. "No way."

"Don't I at least get an interview?" Now her gaze turned mutinous. "That's not fair. I can do it." She spun on her heel and marched toward the front of his office. The space had a tiny lobby, two interior offices and a conference room. Jase loved the location just off Main Street in downtown Crimson.

The receptionist desk had become another place to stack papers since Donna'd left, and as he followed Emily toward the front door he realized how cluttered the area had become. Damn.

She picked up a thin messenger bag from one of the

lobby chairs and pulled out a single sheet of paper. "My résumé," she said, handing it to him. He stared at it, but didn't take it from her. Her mouth thinned. "During college I was an academic assistant for two law school faculty members. I managed calendars, helped with grant proposals and assisted in the preparation of teaching materials. I'm organized and will work hard. I can come in two days this week, and then make my hours closer to full-time once Davey starts school. I'd like to be able to pick him up, but my mom can help out if you need me later in the afternoons."

She kept pushing the résumé toward him, the corners of the paper crumpling against his stomach, so he finally plucked it out of her fingers.

"Emily," he said softly. "I need a legal secretary."

"Right now," she shot back, "you need a warm body that can do dishes."

She had a point, but he wasn't about to admit it.

"I can do this. I can help you." She kept her hands fisted at her sides, her chin notched up. It must have cost her to come to him like this, but Emily still made it seem like she was doing him a favor by demanding he hire her.

"This isn't a job you want." He folded the resume and placed it on the desk. "You're smart and talented—"

"Talented at what?" she asked, breathing out a sad laugh. "Shopping? Planning parties? Not exactly useful skills in Crimson. Or maybe I'm good enough to kiss but not to work for you."

He pointed at the sheet of paper. "You just told me why you're qualified. If you can work for me, you can find another job."

"Don't you think I've tried? I spent this entire morning knocking on doors. I'm a single mom with a son who has special needs, which is a hard sell even if someone did want to hire me." She bit down on her lip. "By the way, they don't. Because I wasn't nice when I was younger and that's what people remember. That's what they see when they look at me."

"I don't."

"You're too nice for your own good," she said, jabbing a finger at him. "That's why I'm here begging." A strangled sound escaped her when she said the word begging. He studied her for crying, but her eyes remained dry. *Thank God.* He couldn't take it if she started crying. "I'm begging, Jase, because I need to know I can support my son. When I left Henry, I wanted out fast so I took nothing. Hell, I'm borrowing my mom's car like I'm a teenager again. I have to start somewhere, but I'm scared I won't be able to take care of Davey on my own. He's about to start kindergarten, but what if something happens? What if he—"

"He's going to be fine, Em." He could see her knuckles turning white even as color rose to her cheeks.

"This was a horrible idea," she muttered, turning her head to stare out onto Main Street as if she couldn't stand to meet his gaze another second. "I'm sorry. I'm a mess."

Jase took a step toward her. It was stupid and self-destructive and a bad idea for both of them, but the truth was he didn't care if Emily was a mess. He wanted her to be his mess.

Emily felt the tips of Jase's fingers on the back of her hand. She couldn't look at him after everything she'd said. All of the shattered pieces of herself she'd just revealed.

But her fingers loosened at his touch, and she wanted to sway into him. Somehow he grounded her and just maybe...

The front door to the office opened, a rush of fresh mountain air breezing over her heated skin. "Jase, you're late."

Emily whirled around to see a short, curvy woman in an ill-fitting silk blouse and shapeless skirt staring at her.

"Sorry," the woman said quickly, glancing between Emily and Jase as she adjusted the bulky purse on her arm. "I didn't realize you had a meeting or..."

"It's fine," Jase told her, stepping away from Emily. "I'll grab my keys, and I'm ready. The Crimson Valley Hiker's Club today, right?"

The woman nodded. "If you're busy—"

He shook his head. "Mari, this is Emily Whitaker. She's Noah's sister and just got back to town. Em, Mari Simpson. Mari works at the library in town but has been kind enough to help keep me on track with my campaign." He gave Mari a warm smile, and Emily's throat tightened. Jase could smile at whomever he wanted. It didn't matter only...

"He'll be a great mayor," Mari chirped with a bright smile of her own. While the woman wasn't classically pretty, the smile softened her features in a way that made her beautiful. "I'm happy to do whatever I can." Her face was sweet and hopeful. The face of a woman who would make a perfect wife. Emily forced herself not to growl in response.

"Keys," Jase said again and disappeared into his office.

Mari continued to smile but it looked forced. "So you're Noah's sister?"

"I am."

"You moved back from Boston, right?"

A simple question but Emily knew it meant that although Mari Simpson wasn't a Crimson native, she'd been downloaded on Emily's past and reputation in town. "Yes," she answered, forcing herself to stay cordial. This was new Emily.

Emily 2.0. Nice Emily.

"It's good to be close to my family and friends again."

Mari tapped a finger to her cheek. "I think I saw your name on the application list for our reference desk opening."

Emily nodded. "I applied at the library."

"Too bad we filled the position already," Mari said a little too sweetly. "Lots of talented people want a chance to live in such a great little town. We only hire people with at least an undergraduate degree. I'm sure you'll find something."

Emily 2.0.

"Thanks for the vote of confidence," she said through clenched teeth. "I think—"

"Emily's going to work for me," Jase said, pocketing his phone and keys as he came back into the room. He kept his gaze trained on Mari.

Her jaw dropped and Emily was pretty sure her own reaction was the same.

"Here? But I've heard… I thought…she's—"

"Organized and hardworking," Jase said, repeating

Emily's words from earlier. "Just what I need to get the office back on track." He patted the tiny woman on the shoulder. "It'll be easier for you, too, Mari. You won't have to keep tabs on me all the time."

She gave a small nod but muttered, "I don't mind."

Finally Jase turned to Emily. "Does tomorrow work for an official start date? I can be here by eight. We'll keep your hours flexible until Davey starts school." For once his eyes didn't reveal any of his feelings. It was as if he hadn't said no and she hadn't broken down in an emotional rant. As if he wasn't offering her this job out of pity.

He held out his hand, palm up. On it sat a shiny gold key. "Just in case you're here before me." He flashed a self-deprecating smile. "Punctuality isn't one of my best qualities."

No, Emily thought, he didn't need to be on time. Jase had more important traits—like the ability to rescue distressed women with a single key.

She should walk away. He knew too much about her now. If there was one thing Emily hated, it was appearing weak. She'd learned to be strong watching her father lose his battle with cancer. She'd married a man who valued power over everything else in his life.

During her divorce she hadn't revealed how scared she'd felt. She'd been strong for Davey. Even when she'd been nothing more than a puddle of uncertainty balled up on the cool tile of the bathroom floor. Every time she got dressed, Emily put her mask into place the same way she pulled on a T-shirt.

But she'd kissed Jase like she wanted to crawl inside his body, then pleaded for a job as if he was her only hope in the world.

When she'd left behind her life in Boston, she'd promised herself she would never depend on a man again. She'd create a life standing on her own two feet, strong and sure.

But maybe strong and sure came after the first wobbly baby step. Maybe…

Forget the self-reflection. Right now she needed a job.

Her pause had been too long, and Jase pulled back his hand, his brown eyes shuttering. She snatched the key at the last moment and squeezed her fingers around it. The metal was warm from his skin and she clutched it to her stomach. "I'll be here in the morning," she told him and with a quick nod to Mari, ducked out of the office before he could change his mind.

A job. She had a job.

She took a deep breath of the sweet pine air. The smell of the forest surrounding Crimson always made her think of her childhood. But now as she walked down the sidewalk crowded with tourists, the town seemed a little brighter than it had been when she'd first returned.

A text came through from her mother, telling her Davey had fallen asleep on the couch so Emily should take her time returning home. What would she do without her mom? She hated asking for help when Meg had recently come through her own health scare, but her mother insisted she loved spending time with her grandson.

Baby steps. A job. Davey starting kindergarten. After things were settled, Emily could think about finding a place of her own. Jase hadn't mentioned a salary, and she didn't care. The job was enough.

The weather was perfect, brilliant blue skies, bright sun and a warm breeze blowing wisps of hair across her cheek. She shrugged out of the suit jacket and folded it over her arm. Just as she walked by a small café, her stomach grumbled.

When was the last time she'd eaten at a restaurant? Not since leaving Boston and then it was always for some law firm party or campaign event. She and Henry hadn't gone on a proper date since their honeymoon. Here in Crimson, Davey liked the quiet and routine of her mother's house.

She sent a quick text to her mom and walked into the restaurant. It was new in town, which she hoped meant unfamiliar people. This space had been a small clothing store the last time she'd been in Crimson. The inside was packed, and she wondered if she'd even get a table in the crowded dining room. It was a disappointment, but not a surprise, when the hostess told her there was nothing available. Just as she turned to leave, someone called her name.

A woman with flaming red hair was waving at her from a booth near the front window.

"You're Emily, right?" the woman asked as she stepped closer. "You must think I'm a crazy stalker, but I recognize you from the Fourth of July Festival. I'm April Sanders, a friend of Katie's."

"The yoga teacher out at Crimson Ranch?"

April nodded. "I got the last empty booth. No pressure, but you're welcome to join me."

Emily thought about declining. She knew Katie had a big group of friends. Hell, everyone in town loved her future sister-in-law. But even though she'd grown up in Crimson, Emily had no one. That's the way she'd wanted it since she got back to town. It was simpler, less mess.

But now the thought of a full meal with adult conversation actually appealed to her. So did spending time with April. The woman was a few years older than Emily but with her gorgeous copper hair and bright green eyes, she looked like she just stepped off the pages of a mountain resort catalog. "Are you sure you don't mind?"

"I'd love it," April said, gesturing to the empty banquette across from her. "It feels strange to be eating alone when there's a crowd waiting for tables."

Emily slid into the booth. "Thank you."

A waitress came by the table almost immediately with a glass of water and another menu. Thankfully, the young woman was a stranger to Emily.

"Are you interested in staying incognito?" April asked when they were alone again. "You looked terrified the waitress might recognize you."

Emily blew out a breath. "I don't have the best reputation in town."

"A sordid past?" April leaned forward and lifted her delicate brows. "Do tell."

"Nothing exciting," Emily answered with a laugh. "Simple story of me thinking I was better than I should have as a girl. Life has a way of slapping you down if you get too big for your britches." She shrugged. "People in small towns like to bear witness to it."

"Life throws out curveballs whether you're big or small," April agreed.

The waitress returned to the table and, as she took

April's order, Emily studied the other woman. April wore no makeup but her fair skin was smooth, and her body fit under a soft pink T-shirt. She looked natural and fresh—perfect for Crimson. After Emily ordered, April smiled. "I met your mom a couple of times at Katie's bakery. She's lovely."

Emily nodded. "One of the most amazing women I know."

"How is she feeling?"

"She gets tired more quickly, but otherwise is back to her normal self. We were lucky the tumor was benign and they could remove it without damaging any other part of her brain."

"She was lucky to have you and Noah come back to help her."

"I wouldn't have been any other place but by her side. That's what family is for, you know?"

"I've heard," April answered softly. "My friend Sara is the closest thing I have to family."

Sara Travers, who ran the guest ranch outside town with her husband, Josh, had moved to Crimson a couple years ago from Los Angeles. Sara had been a famous child star and still acted when the right project came along. Otherwise, she and Josh—a Crimson native and one of Noah's good friends—spent their time managing Crimson Ranch. "Did you come to Crimson with Sara?"

April nodded. "We didn't plan on staying, but then she met Josh and…"

"The rest is history?"

"She had a tough couple of years and deserves this happiness."

"If my brother is any indication, Crimson is *the* place

for happy endings." She smiled. "Have you found your happy-ever-after here?"

"It's a good place to build a life," April said and Emily realized the words weren't an answer to the question.

"Or rebuild a life." The waitress brought their orders, a club sandwich for Emily and a salad for April. Emily leaned across the table. "I like you and I appreciate the invitation to lunch, but after seeing what you eat I'm not sure we can be friends." She pointed to the bowl of dark greens. "Your salad is so healthy I feel guilty picking up a fry from my plate. You don't even have dressing."

The willowy redhead stared at her a long moment and Emily did a mental eye roll. She had the uncanny ability to offend without meaning to by tossing off comments before she thought about them. Her family was used to it and she'd managed to tame the impulse during her marriage but now...

April burst out laughing. "You remind me of Sara. She gives me grief about how I eat, too. I've always been healthy but became more diligent about what I put in my body when I was diagnosed with breast cancer a few years ago."

Emily thumped her palm against her forehead. "Now I feel like an even bigger jerk."

"Don't," April said, still smiling. "I've been cancer-free for over five years."

"My dad died when I was in high school. Pancreatic cancer." She took a bite of sandwich, swallowing around the emotions that always bubbled to the surface when she thought about her father. "I still miss him."

"It's difficult for you being back in Crimson."

"I thought I'd made a life beyond this little town. Returning to Colorado has been an adjustment."

April snagged a fry and popped it in her mouth. "So is divorce."

"Are you..."

"My ex-husband left me during my cancer treatments," April answered. She shrugged. "He couldn't handle me being sick."

"Jerk," Emily muttered.

"And yours?"

"Another jerk." Emily pushed her plate closer to the center of the table, a silent invitation for April to take another fry. When she did, Emily figured this friendship might stand a chance. "I was the one who did the leaving, but it was because my ex couldn't handle that our son wasn't the child he expected or wanted. Henry needed everything to appear perfect, and I bought into the lie."

"And lost yourself in the process?" April's voice was gentle, as if she'd had experience in that area.

Emily bit down on her lip, then nodded.

"I don't have the same history with this town as you, but I can tell you it's a good place to rediscover who you are." April nabbed another fry. "Also to reinvent yourself."

"Is that what you've done?"

"I'm working on it. In addition to Crimson Ranch, I also teach yoga at a studio on the south side of town. You should come in for a class." April leaned closer. "I like you, but I'm not sure I can be friends with someone whose shoulders are so stiff they look like they could crack in half."

Emily laughed, feeling lighter than she had in months. "I may," she told April. "If only to support a friend."

April held up her water glass. "Here's to new friends and new beginnings."

Chapter Five

Jase walked toward the front door of his office at 8:05 the following morning. His tie was slung over his shoulder, his hair still damp from the quick shower he'd taken, but he'd made it almost on time.

Downtown was quiet this early in the morning, one shopkeeper sweeping the sidewalk in front of his store as another arranged a rack of sale clothes. Life Is Sweet bakery would be crowded, so Jase hadn't bothered to stop for his daily dose of caffeine.

He'd been second-, third- and fourth-guessing his decision to offer Emily a job since the words had left his mouth yesterday. He wasn't sure how he was going to handle being so close to her every day, especially when she'd told him their kiss had been a mistake. But he'd also woken up with a sense of anticipation he hadn't felt in years. Not much else could ensure that he was *almost* on time.

He opened the door, then stopped short, checking his watch to make sure he hadn't lost a full day somewhere. The entire space had been transformed. The reception desk was clear other than the papers stacked neatly to one side. The wood furniture in the waiting area had been polished, and the top of the coffee table held a selection of magazines. There was even a plant—one that was green and healthy—on the end table next to the row of chairs where clients waited.

He caught the faint scent of lemon mixed with the richer smell of fresh coffee. His office hadn't looked this good in all the years he'd been here. There was a freshness to the space, as if it had been aired out like a favorite quilt.

He was still taking it all in when Emily appeared from the hallway.

"I hope you don't mind," she said, almost shyly. "I started cleaning up before we talked about how you wanted it done."

He rubbed a hand over his jaw, realizing in his haste to be on time he'd forgotten to shave this morning. "I didn't even know it needed to be done. Are you some kind of a witch who can wiggle her nose and make things happen?" He shook his head. "Because I'm five minutes late and what you've done here looks like it took hours." He glanced at the closed door to his office.

"I didn't touch anything in there. Yet." She reached behind her and shook out her loose bun, blond hair falling over her shoulders. Jase was momentarily mesmerized, but then she gathered the strands and refastened the bun. "I came in early," she told him, moving to stand behind the receptionist's desk.

"How early?"

She moved the stack of papers from one side of the desk to the other before meeting his gaze. "Around five thirty."

"In the morning?" he choked out. "Why were you awake at that time?"

"I don't sleep much," she said with a shrug. "I've gone through the filing system Donna set up and think I understand how it works. We need to talk about how you record billable hours."

He stepped close enough to the desk that his thighs brushed the dark wood. "We need to talk about you not sleeping. How often does that happen?"

"A few times a week," she said quietly. "It's no big deal."

"How many times is a few?"

Her mouth pressed into a thin line. "Why do you care, Jase?"

"How many?"

"Most nights," she answered through clenched teeth. "My doctor in Boston gave me a prescription for pills to help, but I haven't refilled it since I've been back. Davey had trouble adjusting when we first got here, and I wanted to hear him if he needed me."

"And now?"

She shrugged. "I watch him sleep. He's so peaceful, and it makes me happy. This morning my mom's schedule allowed her to watch him for me when he woke up, so I came into the office to get a few things done." She looked up at him, her gaze wary. He noticed something more now, the shadows under her eyes and the tension bracketing her mouth. It didn't lessen her beauty or her effect on him, but he kicked himself that he hadn't seen it before. This woman was exhausted.

"You didn't have to do this," he said, gesturing to the shiny clean space. "But I'm glad you did."

She rewarded him with a small smile. "It was a pit in here, Jase. It's like you don't even care."

"I do care," he argued. "I care about my clients and this town. So what if the office isn't spotless?"

"You're a business owner and you're running for mayor. People have expectations."

He choked out a laugh. "Tell me about it." He didn't mind taking grief from her because the brightness had returned to her gaze. The Emily he remembered from high school had been so sure of herself and her place in this world. She'd held on to that pretense since returning to Crimson, but the more time he spent with her the more he could see the fragile space between the cracks in her armor. A part of him wanted to rip away all of her defenses because they were guarding things that held her heart captive. But he hated seeing her troubled and knew she hated revealing any weakness.

"Thank you for this job. I know you didn't want to hire me."

No. He wanted to kiss her and hold her and take care of her. The kissing and holding weren't going to be helped by working with her, but he could take care of her and that was a start.

"You were right," he admitted. "I needed help. There are too many things on my plate right now, so I've been ignoring the office. It's starting to show in my work, and that's not going to help anyone."

"The town loves you. They'll cut you some slack."

"They love what I do for them."

"You do too much."

He shook his head. "There's no such thing. Not for someone with my history."

"The Crenshaw family history isn't yours, Jase. The weight of a generations-old reputation shouldn't rest on one man's shoulders."

If only that were true. "My dad isn't going to help carry the load." He didn't want to talk about this. Emily was here so he could help her, not the other way around. "I have to be at the courthouse at nine, so we should talk about what else needs to be done. I'm going to get a cup of coffee first, and you're an angel for making it. For all of this. Thank you, Em."

She tapped one finger on the screen of the desktop computer. "Eight thirty."

"Already?" He glanced at his watch.

"No, you have to be at the courthouse at eight thirty." She moved around the desk, her hips swaying under the fitted cropped pants she wore. She'd paired them with a thin cotton sweater in a pale yellow along with black heels. It was more casual than yesterday but still professional. "I'll get your coffee."

"You don't have to—"

"I want to." She tipped up her chin, as if daring him to contradict her. "So you can get ready to go."

Before he could argue, she disappeared around the corner.

This place wasn't good enough for someone like Emily. His office, even though it was clean, was too shabby for her crisp elegance. He imagined that she'd fit perfectly into the upper echelons of Boston society. Emily looked like a lady who lunched, a fancy wife who could chair events and fund-raisers and never have a hair out of place. Yet as he followed her, he watched wisps of blond hair try to escape from the knot at the back of her head.

She poured coffee into a travel mug, and Jase was momentarily distracted by the fact that the clean dishes and coffee mugs were put away on the shelf above the utility sink.

Emily turned, thrusting the stainless steel mug toward him. Her fingers were pink from the water and had several paper cuts on the tips. Not as delicate as she looked, his Emily.

No. Not his. Not even for a minute.

But she was here. Although he'd done her a favor, he needed her. He wanted her. Any way he could have her.

"You're welcome in my office while I'm gone." He brushed a lock of hair behind her ear and felt a small amount of satisfaction when she sucked a breath. "I should be back by noon."

"You have a meeting with Toby Jenkins here at one thirty."

He nodded, thankful he'd set up the calendars on his cell phone and office computers to sync automatically. He was in the habit of entering meetings in his calendar, but that didn't mean he remembered to check it every day.

"I told my mom I'd be home by two today. Davey still naps in the afternoons, and I like to be there when he wakes up."

"I can pick up lunch on my way back. Any requests?"

"You don't need to—"

"It's the least I can do, Emily. The way you transformed the office went beyond anything Donna could have done. It feels good not to be surrounded by my usual mess."

One side of her mouth curved. "I'm glad to be useful."

What had her ex-husband done to beat down the spirited girl he'd known into this brittle, unsure woman? Jase wasn't a fighter, but he would have liked to punch Henry Whitaker.

Instead, he gave Emily a reassuring smile. "You're the best."

Her smile dimmed, but before he could figure out why, she tapped her watch. "You need to go or you're going to be late."

"They're used to me being late."

"Not with me running the show." She pointed to the door. "Now go. I've got your inner sanctum to tackle."

He laughed, then wished her luck and headed back out into the bright sunshine. It was the best start to a morning he'd had in ages.

By the time he parked in front of his father's trailer a few minutes before noon, Jase's mood had disintegrated into a black hole of frustration. Even though he expected it from Emily's text, seeing the Crawfords' 4Runner at the side of the mobile home only made it worse.

He didn't want Emily here. This part of his life was private, protected. Most people in town knew his father, or knew of him if they'd lived in Crimson long enough. But even as a kid, Jase had never let anyone visit the run-down home where he'd lived. Not even Noah.

He stood on the crumbling front step for a moment trying to rein in his clamoring emotions. Then he heard Emily's laughter spill out from the open window and pushed through the door.

Her back was to him as she faced the tiny counter

in the kitchen. "Canned spaghetti is not real food," she said with another laugh.

"It's real food if I eat it and like it," his dad growled in response, but there was humor in his tone. His father sat in one of the rickety wooden chairs at the table. He watched Emily like she was some sort of mystical being come to life inside his tumbledown home.

"I'm not a great cook," she shot back, "but even I can make homemade meatballs. I'll teach you." He could see she was dumping the can of bright red sauce and pasta into a ceramic bowl.

"If we're having Italian night," his dad said, pronouncing Italian with a long *I*, "you'd best bring a bottle of wine with you."

Jase let the door slam shut at that moment. Emily whirled to face him, her smile fading as she took in his expression. Declan shifted in the chair, his own smile growing wider.

"Just in time for lunch," his dad said, even though he knew how much Jase hated any food that came from a can.

"How was the courthouse?" Emily covered the bowl with a paper towel and put it in the microwave shoved in the corner of the counter.

Taking a breath, he caught Emily's scent overlaid with the stale smell of the trailer. The combination was an assault on his senses. The hold he had on his emotions unleashed as he stalked forward, shouldering Emily out of the way to punch in a minute on the microwave timer. "What the hell are you doing here?" he asked, crowding her against the kitchen sink.

"My fault," his father said from behind him. "I forgot I had a doctor's appointment this morning. When you didn't answer your cell phone, I called the office. Emily explained you were unavailable but was nice enough to drive me."

Jase looked over his shoulder. "You should have rescheduled the appointment."

"It wasn't a problem," Emily said. "Your office was organized and I—"

"I offered you a job as a legal secretary," he bit out. "That's work with professional boundaries. Inserting yourself into my personal life isn't part of the job description."

Those blue eyes that had been so warm and full of life iced over in a second. He expected her to argue but instead her lips pressed together and a moment later she whispered, "My bad. Won't happen again."

"Jase, what's crawled up your butt?" his dad asked, his voice booming in the tense silence that had descended between him and Emily.

She lifted one eyebrow. "I'm not going to stick around to find out." Skirting around him, she gave Declan a quick hug. "Enjoy your spaghetti. I'm going to hold you to that cooking lesson. But grape juice, no wine."

"Thank you, darlin'." His dad's voice softened. "You're a good girl. I'm sorry about this."

"It's not on you," she whispered.

Jase didn't turn around, his hands pressed hard to the scarred Formica. He heard the creak of the door as it opened and shut, not the angry bang he expected but a soft click that tore a hole in his gut. Still he didn't move.

The chair scraped as his father stood. He moved behind Jase to take the bowl out of the microwave. For several minutes the only sound was the spoon clinking and the rustle of a newspaper.

"She doesn't belong here," Jase said finally, rubbing his hand over his face as he turned. "Emily works for me now. That's all, Dad. She isn't part of this."

"That girl has been a part of you for years," Declan answered, setting down the spoon in the empty bowl.

Jase felt his eyes widen before he could stop the reaction. He'd never talked to anyone, especially his father, about his feelings for Emily. He understood Noah knew but had never spoken it aloud.

"I'm a bad drunk," Declan said with a shrug. "But I was never blind, and you're my son. I know you better than you think."

"Emily's in a rough place now. I'm helping her get back on her feet. That's all."

"You're embarrassed about me and how you grew up."

Another bit of unspoken knowledge better left in the shadows. "You're in a better place, Dad. I'm proud of you for staying sober."

Declan choked out a laugh. "I'm the one who's proud, Jase. But you take on too much that isn't yours. My reputation and our family history. The way you were raised. You've overcome a lot, and you don't need to be ashamed of it. You don't have to make it all better."

Jase thought about his ancestor's picture in the town jail and how he wanted his family legacy to be something more than it was. "If you won't let me move you to a better house, I respect that decision. But I don't want her here. You need to respect that."

"From what I can tell, Emily Crawford is plenty capable of making her own decisions."

But she was *working* for him now. It was what she'd wanted, and it changed things. Not his need or desire, but his inclination to act on it. "Her name is Emily *Whitaker*, Dad. She was married. She has a son. Neither one of us is who we were before."

His father smiled. "I think that's the point."

Chapter Six

Emily looked up from the old rocker on her mother's front porch at the sound of a car coming down the gravel driveway. It was almost nine at night, and Davey had been asleep close to an hour.

She hadn't expected her mother to return from her date with Max Moore so soon. But when Emily recognized Jase's Jeep, her first inclination was to run to the house and shut the door.

He'd hurt her today, and she hated that anyone—any man—had the power to do that. While she understood that Jase's reaction had been about his own issues, a part of her still took the blame he'd placed on her. Her faults sometimes felt so obvious it was easy to hold herself accountable for any perceived slight. Flawed as she might be, Emily had never been a coward.

So she remained on the rocker, her legs curled under

the thin blanket she'd brought out to ward off the evening chill of the high mountains. Although she couldn't concentrate on the actual words, she kept her eyes trained on the e-reader in her lap as a door slammed shut and the heavy footfall of boots sounded on the steps.

"What are you reading?"

She ran one finger over the screen of the e-reader but didn't answer.

"You can ignore me," he said as he sank into the chair next to her, "but I won't go away."

"There's always hope," she quipped, her fingers gripping the leather cover of the e-reader tighter at his soft chuckle.

They sat in silence for a minute, and Emily's grasp began to relax. As if sensing it he said, "I'm sorry, Em."

"It's fine," she lied. "Point taken. I overstepped the bounds." There she went, instinctively making his mistake her fault.

"My reaction wasn't about you. What you did for my dad today was kind. It made him happier than I've seen him in a long time to have a beautiful woman caring for him."

"No big deal."

"Don't do that." His hand was around her wrist, warmth seeping through the fleece sweatshirt she'd pulled on when the sun disappeared behind the mountain. "It was special to him, and it should have been to me, as well." He stood, releasing her, and paced to the edge of the porch. "I love my father, but I hate the man he was when I was younger. He was mean and embarrassing. Everyone knew the problems he had, but that didn't stop me from being humiliated when I'd have to get him home after a night at the bars."

She could see the tension in his shoulders as he gazed out into the darkening night. "He showed up one year for a parent-teacher conference so drunk he ended up puking all over the first-floor bathroom. I never let him come to another school function."

She flipped closed the cover of her e-reader, her heart already melting for this man's pain. "Jase—"

He turned to her, folded his arms across his chest. "It killed me to live in that trailer growing up. The only saving grace was that no one but me had to see him at his worst. Even Noah, all the times he picked me up, has never been inside. That place represents my greatest shame, and my dad refuses to move. To see you there with all of the memories that seem to seep out of the walls to choke me... I couldn't stand it. It felt like you'd be contaminated by it."

Emily stood, placed the blanket and e-reader on the chair and walked toward him.

Jase shook his head. "You're too good for that, Em. Too good for him. I'm sorry I lashed out, but I still hate that you—that anyone—has seen that piece of who I am."

"No." She stepped into his space until she could feel his breath whispering over the top of her head. "You're too good to give in to that shame. Where you came from doesn't change who you are now."

"Are you kidding?" He didn't move away from her but leaned back against the porch rail as if he needed space. "That trailer and what it represents *made* me who I am. The night in my front yard, you said I was perfect, and I know what my reputation is around town. Nice Jase. Sweet Jase. Perfect Jase. No one sees anything else because I don't let them. Everyone thinks I work so damn hard despite my family's reputation in Crimson. I work hard *because* of where I came from. Because I'm scared to death if I don't, the poison that has crushed the self-respect of so many people in my family will take me down, too."

Something dark and dangerous flashed in his eyes and she saw who he was under the Mr. Perfect veneer he'd spent years polishing to a bright shine. He was a man at the edge of his control and a part of her wanted him to shuck off his restraint. With her. Yes. She could handle it. She would welcome whatever he had to offer.

He blinked, and the moment was gone. His chest rose and fell like he'd sprinted up Crimson Mountain. She placed her hand on it, fingers splayed, and felt his heartbeat thrumming under her touch. "You aren't your father." She said the words softly and felt his breath hitch. "I know what it's like to want to prove something so badly it makes you into someone you're not. Someone fake and false. You're real, Jase. Not perfect. Real."

"I'm sorry," he said again, lifting his palm to press it over her hand. "For what I said and how I treated you."

She let a small smile curve her lips. "I think this makes us even."

"You did good today. In my office and with my dad. Thank you."

This was the part where she should step away. If they were even, it was a fresh start. But she couldn't force herself to move. Emily might not believe in perfect, but she had learned to appreciate real. The knowledge that Jase was different than she'd assumed both humbled and excited her. Of all people, she should have known not to judge a person by who they were on the outside.

She'd built an entire life on outward impressions only to watch it crumble around her.

The connection she felt with Jase, her awareness of him, suddenly flared to life stronger than it had before. She moved her hand up his chest and around to the back of his neck. At the same time she lifted onto her tiptoes so she could press her mouth to his. He tasted like night air and mint gum, and she loved how much he could communicate simply through the pressure of his mouth on hers.

He angled his head and ran his tongue across her bottom lip. His hands came to rest on her hips, pulling her closer until the front of her was plastered against him. Unlike other men she'd known, he didn't rush the kiss. It was as if learning her bit by bit was enough for him. He savored every taste, trailing kisses along her jaw before nipping at her earlobe.

"Your ears are sensitive," he whispered when she moaned softly. His breath feathered against her skin. "You touch them when you're nervous."

"I don't," she started to argue, then he bit down on the lobe again and she squirmed. "You're observant," she amended.

"I want more. I want to know everything about you," he said and claimed her mouth again.

Her brain was fuzzy but the meaning of his words penetrated the fog of desire after a few moments. "No." She lifted her head and tried to step away but he held her steady.

"Why?" A kiss against her jaw.

"I can't think when you do that."

"Then I'll do it more."

She opened her mouth to argue, and he took the opportunity to deepen the kiss. One thing she'd say for Jase Crenshaw—the man was persistent. Even though she knew she should stop it, she gave in to the need building inside her. Her body sang with desire, tremors skittering over her skin. Jase ran his fingers up under the hem of her sweatshirt and across her spine. Everywhere he touched her Emily burned. Her breasts were heavy and sensitive where they rubbed against his T-shirt and she wanted more.

So much more.

So much it scared her into action. As Jase's hands moved to the front of her waist and brushed the swell of her breasts, she wrenched away from him. With unsteady hands, she grabbed on to the front porch rail to prevent herself from moving back to the warmth she already missed.

"We've determined I'm not perfect," Jase said, his tone a mix of amusement and frustration. "So what's the problem now?"

"I work for you."

"Are you asking to be fired?"

She glanced at him and saw he was teasing. Her shoulders relaxed. "I don't want to complicate things, Jase. I know you gave me the job because you felt sorry for me and this…" She pointed between the two of them. "Would only muddy the waters more."

"I don't feel sorry for you." He came closer and she didn't resist when he cupped her face in his hands. "I respect you, and I want you. But neither of those emotions involves pity."

"Why are you running for mayor?"

His hands dropped to his sides. "I think I can help

the town move forward. I've been on city council long enough to understand what needs to be done and—"

"You have a responsibility," she finished for him.

"You say that like it's a bad thing."

"It's not, but your life is filled with obligations. I don't want to be another one."

"You're—"

"I'd like to be your friend."

He stared at her for several seconds, then blew out a breath. "I'd like that, too, but it doesn't have to mean—"

"Yes, it does," she interrupted, not bothering to hide her smile at the crushed puppy-dog look of disappointment he gave her.

With a small nod, he moved around her. "Good night, Emily."

"Good night, Jase." She watched his taillights disappear into the darkness, then turned for the house. For the first time in forever, she fell asleep within minutes of her head hitting the pillow.

Friday morning, Jase walked the three blocks from his office to the Crimson Community Center and thought about how nice it was not to be rushing through town. He was speaking to the downtown business coalition and probably would have been late for the meeting if Emily hadn't shoved him out the door.

She was a stickler for punctuality, something that had never been a strength of his. He cared about being on time, but he often got so lost in whatever he was doing that he stopped paying attention to anything else. She hadn't been in the office yesterday, and despite how organized she'd left things on Wednesday, he'd found he missed knowing she was sharing his space.

She was a distraction but the best kind possible, and now he spent the minutes going over what he planned to say to the group of business owners. Ever since Emily had asked the question, Jase had been pondering the answer to why he was running for mayor. It wasn't as if he didn't have enough to keep him busy with his law practice.

He came around the corner and noticed Mari pacing in front of the entrance to the community center. Automatically he checked his watch, since his one campaign worker tended to pace when she was anxious.

"We have a problem," she said, adjusting her heavy-rimmed glasses as she strode toward him.

He held up his hands. "I'm not scheduled to speak for another ten minutes. It's good."

"Your opponent got here first," she answered, shaking her head. "It's *really* bad, Jase."

"What opponent?"

"Charles Thompson."

Jase's stomach dropped to the pavement like a cement brick. "Charles Thompson isn't running for mayor. I'm unopposed in the election."

"Not anymore. He has the signatures he needs to put his name on the ballot and filed as a candidate with the courthouse before yesterday's deadline. I don't understand why he's doing this."

"Because it's me." Jase rubbed a hand over his eyes. "Charles has been at loose ends since he retired as sheriff. I bet my dad called and rubbed the election in his face. If there's anything the Thompsons can't stand, it's a Crenshaw getting ahead."

"That's plain spiteful."

Spiteful and stupid and why was he doing this again?

Because he owed it to the town? Because he had some-thing to prove?

"You have to get in there and prove you're a better candidate." Mari tugged on his arm, but Jase stood his ground. He didn't want to face Charles and everything the older man knew about his childhood. If there was one person who knew where all the Crenshaw skeletons were hidden, it was Charles Thompson. "Jase, let's go."

He could walk away right now, withdraw his can-didacy. Charles would be a fine mayor, maybe even better than Jase. The older man had nothing but time to devote to the job. But if Jase won, maybe he could stop trying so hard to make amends for a past he didn't own. Perhaps it would finally be enough—he would be enough—to excise the ghosts of his past.

Jase wasn't his father or any of the infamous men in his family. He'd paid more than his dues; he'd tried to atone for every sin committed by someone with the last name Crenshaw. Now was his time to bury the past for good. He couldn't walk away.

Taking a deep breath, he straightened his tie and smoothed his fingers over the hair curling at the nape of his neck. A haircut was still on the to-do list, right after fighting for his right to lead this town.

He followed Mari into the crowded meeting room where Charles Thompson stood at the podium. A ruth-less light snapped in his eyes as he met Jase's gaze over the heads of the members of the coalition. Jase knew he had friends in this room, but facing Sheriff Thomp-son turned him into the scared, cowering boy he'd been years ago. He'd dreaded seeing the patrol car parked in front of his dad's trailer and knowing what it meant.

Those days were a distant memory for most people,

Declan Crenshaw having faded into the background of the Crimson community. But for Jase they were like a razor across an open wound—raw and painful.

"My esteemed opponent has arrived," Charles announced into the microphone, his deep voice booming through the room.

People in the audience turned to where Jase stood at the back and he forced a neutral look on his face. He made eye contact with a couple of friends, Katie Garrity, who was representing her bakery, and Josh Travers from Crimson Ranch. Katie gave him a sympathetic smile and Josh looked almost as angry as Jase felt.

Their support bolstered his confidence but his courage took a nosedive at Thompson's next words. "Come on up here, boy," Charles said, his gaze boring in Jase's taught nerves. "I want to talk to you about the future of this town and family values."

Jase banged through the front door of his office an hour after he'd left, holding on to his temper by the thinnest thread. Emily jumped in her chair, glancing up from the computer screen.

"How did it go?"

"Fine," he bit out, not stopping. He could feel the mask he wore beginning to crumble and needed the safety of being behind a closed door when it did. "I have a meeting with Morris Anderson at eleven. Let me know when he gets here."

He dropped his briefcase on the floor, slammed his office door shut behind him and stalked to the window behind his desk, trying to get his breathing under control as he stared out to the parking lot in back of the building.

"All those slamming doors don't sound like *fine* to me."

He didn't bother turning at Emily's cool voice behind him. "Do you understand what a closed door means?" he asked.

"Better than you'd imagine," she answered with a small laugh. "But in this case, I don't care. Either you tell me what happened at the meeting, or I can call Katie. Which do you prefer?"

Jase closed his eyes and concentrated on making his lungs move air in and out. He knew there were no secrets in Crimson, at least not for long. His phone had started ringing and beeping with incoming calls and texts as soon as he walked out of the community center.

"Charles Thompson is running against me for mayor. He announced his candidacy to the downtown coalition this morning."

She didn't say anything, and Jase finally turned. Emily stood just inside the doorway to his office. After his secretary retired, Jase convinced himself that he preferred running the entire office on his own. So much of his life was filled with people and responsibility. This space had become a sanctuary of sorts, a place where he was in total control. He answered to no one.

In only a few days, Emily's presence had become the answer to a secret need he didn't know how to voice. Not only was she organized and efficient, but she breathed new life into an existence that had become so predictable Jase couldn't seem to force its path out of the familiar ruts.

This morning she wore a simple cotton dress with a light sweater thrown over her shoulders and strappy sandals. Her hair was held back with a clip but the length of it tumbled over her shoulders. The scent of her shampoo mixed with perfume tangled in the air, and Jase had noticed on Wednesday the hint of it lingered even after she left for the day.

"So what?" she asked when he finally met her gaze. "You've done more for this town than Charles Thompson. People love you."

He shook his head. "He was sheriff," he told her, as if that explained everything. The word *sheriff* captured the past Jase had worked so hard to bury under the duty and responsibility he shouldered in town.

"You've been the de facto leader on town council for several years. Noah told me you were instrumental in convincing Liam Donovan to move his company's headquarters to Crimson."

She stepped farther into the room and, like he was magnetized, Jase moved around the desk toward her. Toward the certainty of her unmistakable beauty and the sound of her voice. Maybe if he listened to her long enough, he could believe in himself the way she seemed to.

"From what I remember, Thompson was a decent sheriff, but this town has never had a big problem with crime. Business and keeping things moving forward have been a struggle for some of the older generation. Things are different now than when I left, and people say you're the reason."

If only it were that simple. "He knows everything about me."

Her delicate brows came down, as if she couldn't understand the significance of what he was saying.

"Charles ran the department when we were kids," he explained. "During the time when my grandpa died and Mom left with Sierra. My dad was still working at the mine, and he was at his lowest. It was worse than anyone knows." He paused, cleared his throat to expel the emotions threatening his airways. "Except Charles. He knows every sordid detail."

"That past has nothing to do with you."

"That past *is* me," he argued.

She shook her head. "Charles can't use anything he knows because of his position as sheriff in this election."

"He already has. Most of what he talked about at today's meeting was family values. He had his wife of thirty-four years and his two sons sitting in the front row. Hell, Miriam brought muffins to hand out."

"You want muffins? Katie will make you dozens of them. We can hand out baked goods to every voter in this town."

"That's not the point. You know how perception plays into politics. He's sowed the seeds of doubt about me. Now people will start talking…about me and my family and our history in Crimson."

"They'll understand he's running a smear campaign."

"No, they won't." He ran his hands through his hair, squeezed shut his eyes. "He was so smooth. Charles actually talked about how much he admired me, how much I'd overcome. He claimed he'd always felt protective of me because my mother abandoned me and my dad was so messed up. Would you believe he even compared me to his own sons?"

"Aaron and Todd?" Emily snorted. "Those two caused more trouble as teens than anyone else in the school. I haven't seen Todd, but from what I can tell, Aaron hasn't changed a bit. He's still a big bully. I don't know how many times I have to say no to a date before he quits calling me."

"He's calling you?" As angry as Jase was about Charles, temper of a different sort flared to the surface of his skin, hot and prickly. It was almost a relief to channel his frustration toward something outside himself. Something he could control. Above all else, Jase understood the value of control. "I'll take care of it."

"Hold on there, Hero-man. I don't need you to handle Aaron for me. I can take care of annoying jerks all on my own."

"You can handle everything, right?"

He regretted the rude question as soon as it was out of his mouth. Emily should snap back at him because he was lashing out at her with no cause. Instead, she flashed him a saucy grin. "Takes one to know one."

The smile, so unexpected and undeserved, diffused most of his anger, leaving him with a heaping pile of steaming self-doubt. He sat on the edge of his desk and leaned forward, hands on his knees.

"I'm sorry. I know you can take care of yourself." His chin dropped to his chest and he stared at the small stain peeking out from under one of the chairs in front of the desk. "But it's a lot easier to worry about other people than think of how quickly my own life is derailing."

A moment later he felt cool fingers brush away the hair from his forehead. He wanted to lean into her touch but forced himself to remain still. "Did you ever meet Andrew Meyer who used to run this office? I took over his practice four years ago, and I haven't changed a thing." He pushed the toe of his leather loafer against the chair leg until the stain was covered. "Not one piece of furniture or painting on the wall. You can still see the frame marks from where he took down his law school diploma and I never bothered to replace it with mine. I inherited his secretary and his clients, and I haven't lifted a finger to make this place my own. Hell, I think the magazines in the lobby are probably four years old. Maybe even older."

"I switched them for current issues," she said softly.

Her fingers continued to caress him and it felt so damn good to take a small amount of comfort from her. Too good. He lifted his head, and she dropped her hand.

"Why haven't you changed anything?" She didn't move away, and it was the hardest thing Jase had ever done not to pull her closer.

"Because this place isn't mine."

"It is," she said, her tone confused. "It's your office. Your clients. Your reputation." She laughed. "Your mortgage."

"This is the oldest law practice in the town. It was founded in the early 1900s and passed down through the Meyer family for generations. Andrew didn't have kids, so he offered a partnership position to me when I was still in law school. He wanted a Crimson native to take over the firm. This is his legacy. Not mine."

"Jase, you are the poster child for the town's favorite son. Charles Thompson can't hold a candle to the man you've become. Whether it was despite where you came from or because of it, the truth doesn't change."

"What if who people see isn't the truth? What if I've become too good at playing the part people expect of me?"

"You don't have to reflect the town's image of you back at them. You're more than a two-dimensional projection of yourself. Show everyone who you really are."

Staring into Emily's crystal-blue eyes, it was tempting. The urge to throw it all away, create the life he wanted, curled around his senses until the freedom of it was all he could see, hear and taste. Right behind the whisper of release came a pounding, driving fear that cut him off at the knees.

Who he was, who he'd been before he'd started down the path to redeeming his family name was a lost, lonely, scared boy. The memories he'd secreted away in the parts of his soul where he didn't dare look threatened to overtake him.

He stood abruptly, sending Emily stumbling back a few steps. "I'm going to win this election. I need people to see the best version of me, not the grubby kid Charles remembers."

Her eyes were soft. "Jase."

"I've worked toward this for years. It's what people expect..." He paused, took a breath. "It's what I want."

"Are you sure?"

"Charles isn't right for this. I'm going to be mayor."

She placed a light hand on his arm. "I'm going to help you."

He looked at her elegant fingers wrapped around his shirtsleeve. "Because you work for me."

"Because we're friends."

His eyes drifted shut for a moment. "Right. I forgot."

He felt a poke at his ribs. "Liar."

She had no idea. "I saw Katie at the meeting," he told her, needing to lighten the mood. He was too raw to go down that road with Emily. As much as he craved her kiss, he couldn't touch her again and not reveal the depth of his feelings. He thought he could control how much he needed her, but not when he was carrying his heart in his hands, ready to offer it to her if she asked. "She asked about plans for the bachelor and bachelorette parties."

Emily pulled a face. "No strippers."

He laughed in earnest. "I wasn't even thinking that."

"All men think that."

"You've got the whole male population figured out?"

"Like I said before, you're not complicated."

When it came to Emily, he wished it were true. His feelings for the woman standing in front of him had been simple for years. He wanted her. An unattainable crush. Unrequited love. End of story.

But a new chapter had started since she'd returned to town, and it was tangled in ways Jase couldn't take the time to unravel. Not if he was going to stay the course to his duty to Crimson.

"Then we're talking beer and poker night?"

Emily opened her mouth, then glanced over her shoulder as the door to the outer office opened. "Your appointment's here."

"Admit it, you like beer and poker."

She shook her head. "Come over for dinner tonight and we'll brainstorm better options." Her hand flew to cover her mouth as if she was shocked she'd extended the invitation.

"Yes," he said before she could retract the offer. "What time?"

Emily blinked. "Six."

"I'll be there."

"Jason, are you here?" a frail voice yelled from the front office.

"In my office, Mr. Anderson," Jase called. "Come on back."

"I should go…um…"

"Finish editing the brief I gave you?" Jase suggested, keeping his expression solemn.

"Exactly," she agreed.

As Morris Anderson tottered into the room, Emily said hello to the older man and disappeared.

"That Meg Crawford's girl?" Morris asked after she'd gone. Morris was here to revise the terms of his will, which he did on a monthly basis just to keep his four children on their toes.

Jase nodded, taking a seat behind his desk.

"I went to school with her grandmother back in the day. Spunky little thing."

"Good to know where Emily gets it." Jase pulled out Morris's bulging file. "Who made you angry this month?"

"Who didn't make me angry?" Morris asked through a coughing fit. "My kids are ungrateful wretches, but I love them." He pointed to the door, then to Jase. "The spunky ones are trouble," he said after a moment.

"Do you think so?" Jase felt his hackles rise. His protective inclination toward Emily was a palpable force surrounding him.

"I know so," Morris answered with a nod. "Trouble of the best kind. A man needs a little spunk to keep things interesting."

"I'd have to agree, Mr. Anderson," he said with a smile. "I'd definitely have to agree."

Chapter Seven

Emily wasn't sure how long she'd been sitting on the hallway floor when a pair of jeans and cowboy boots filled her line of sight.

"Emily?" Jase crouched down in front of her, placed a gentle hand on her knee. "What's wrong, sweetheart?"

"Nothing," she whispered. "Except dinner might be a little delayed. Sorry. I didn't realize you were here."

"I could see you through the screen door. I knocked but…"

"Hi, Jase." Davey's voice was sweet. Her boy didn't seem the least concerned to see his mother having a meltdown on the hardwood floor. "I built the space station hospital. Want to see it?"

"In a minute, buddy," Jase told him. "I'm going to hang out here with your mom first."

She tried to offer her son a smile but her face felt brittle. "Are you getting hungry, Davey?"

"Not yet." Small arms wrapped around her shoulders. "It's alright, Mama." The hug lasted only a few seconds but it was enough to send her already tattered emotions into overdrive. If her son was voluntarily giving her a hug, she must be in really bad shape.

She expelled a breath as Davey went back into the office. The tremors started along her spine but quickly spread until it felt like her whole body shook.

"Let's get you off the floor." Jase didn't wait for an answer. He scooped her into his arms and carried her toward the family room. Jase was strong and steady, the ends of his hair damp like he'd showered before coming over. She breathed in the scent of his shampoo mixed with the clean, woodsy smell she now associated with him alone. How appropriate that the man who was the poster child for Crimson would smell like the forest. As much as she wanted to sink into his embrace, Emily remained stiff against him. If she let go now, she might really lose it. "Where's your mom?"

"Book club," she managed between clenched teeth. "We should probably reschedule dinner for another night."

"I'm not leaving you like this." He deposited her onto the couch. "Not until you tell me what's going on."

Emily fought to pull herself together. She was so close to the edge it was as if she could feel the tiny spikes of hysteria pricking at the backs of her eyes. The cushions of the couch were soft and worn from years of movie nights and Sundays watching football. She wanted to curl up in a ball and ignore the constant pounding life seemed determined to serve up to her.

She couldn't look at Jase and risk him seeing the humiliation she knew was reflected in her eyes. She stood, moving around the couch in the opposite direction. The kitchen opened to the family room, separated by a half wall and the dining room table. "I'd planned to make steaks," she said quickly, ignoring the trembling in her fingers. "But I didn't get them out of the freezer, so we may be stuck with hot dogs. Do you mind turning on the grill?"

He let himself out onto the flagstone patio as she opened the pantry door and scanned the contents of the cupboard. She heard him return a few minutes later but kept her attention on the cupboard. "How do you feel about boxed mac and cheese? I don't know how Mom managed to make a home-cooked meal every night when we were younger. She worked part-time, drove us around to after-school activities, and still we had family dinners most evenings. You remember, right? She loved cooking for you and Noah."

He was standing directly behind her when she turned, close enough she was afraid he might reach for her. And if he did, she might shatter into a million tiny fragments of disappointment and regret. "I know I'm babbling. It's a coping mechanism. Give me a pass on this one, Jase."

His dark eyes never wavered. "What happened?"

Her fingers tightened on the small cardboard box so hard the corners bent. "An overreaction to some news. My meltdown is over. I'm fine."

"What news?"

"Does it matter?" She shook her head. "I lost the privilege of a major freak-out when I became a mother. Moms don't have a lot of time for wallowing when dinner is late."

"Tell me anyway."

She slammed the box of mac and cheese on the counter, then bent to grab a pot out of a lower cabinet. "I liked you better when you were nice and easygoing and not all up in my business."

Elbowing him out of the way she turned on the faucet and filled the pot with water. "Apparently, my ex-husband got remarried last weekend. One of my former friends in Boston was nice enough to text me a photo from the wedding."

She set the pot of water on the stove and turned on the burner. The poof of sound as it ignited felt like the dreams she'd had for her life. There one minute and then up in flames. "It was small—nothing like the extravaganza I planned—only family and close friends."

She laughed. "My friends are now her friends. She was a campaign worker. What a cliché." She glanced over her shoulder, unable to stop speaking once she'd started. "You know the best part? She's pregnant. A shotgun wedding for Henry Whitaker III. It's like Davey and I never existed. We're gone and he's remaking our life with someone else. Our exact damn life."

"I'm sorry."

"Don't be sorry." She ripped off the top of the box with so much force that an explosion of dried macaroni noodles spilled across the counter. "I'm not."

"You don't have to pretend with me."

"I'm not sorry, Jase. I'm mad. It's mostly self-directed. I let myself be sucked into that life. I was so busy pretending I couldn't even see Henry for who he was." She scooped up the stray noodles, dropped them in the water and then dumped the rest of the box's contents in with them. "My son has to pay the price."

"Your ex-husband is an idiot."

"To put it mildly."

"There are other words going through my mind," Jase said, his tone steely. "But I'm not going to waste my energy on a man so stupid he would let you go and give up his son because of a political image."

Emily took a deep breath and released it along with much of her tension. "I don't miss him." It had been a shock to get the text about Henry but she hadn't been lying to Jase when she told him she was most angry at herself. "How did I marry a man who I can feel nothing but revulsion for five months after leaving him?"

"He hurt you," Jase answered simply.

"I should have seen him for who he was. My parents had a good marriage. There was so much love in this house."

He reached out, traced a fingertip along her jaw. "There was also a lot of pain when your dad died."

"Yes, and it left scars on all of us. But Noah managed to fall in love with an amazing woman. Mom is now dating someone who makes her happy. I seem to be the one with horrible taste."

Jase smiled. "Did you meet any of the women your brother dated before Katie?"

"From what I've heard, *date* is a fairly formal term for Noah's pre-Katie relationships."

"Exactly."

"He's one of the lucky ones." She sighed and stepped away from Jase. Staring into his dark eyes made her forget he wasn't for her. Jase Crenshaw was all about duty and responsibility. Whether he was willing to admit it or not, his image was a big part of his identity. He wasn't motivated by the hunger for power and prestige that had influenced her ex-husband. But it didn't change the fact he would eventually want more than Emily was willing to give.

She opened the refrigerator and grabbed a pack of hot dogs from the shelf. "Man the grill, Mr. Perfect. We're eating like kids tonight."

Jase watched her for a long, heavy moment before his lips curved into a grin. "The only thing perfect about me is my grilling skills."

She smiled in return, knowing he'd given her a pass. Maybe he'd sensed her frazzled emotions couldn't take any more deep conversation. "Let's see if your hot dogs can beat my mac and cheese."

"I'm up for the challenge," he said and let himself out onto the patio.

Alone in the kitchen, Emily went to check on her son. He was still busy with his Lego structures and she watched him for a few minutes before giving him a fifteen-minute warning for dinner. Davey's difficulty with rapid transitions had driven Henry crazy. Her ex-husband had loved spontaneity when he wasn't working or campaigning. A game of pick up football with the neighbors, a bike ride into town for dinner or an impromptu weekend at the shore. Henry had to be moving at all times, his energy overpowering and bordering on manic.

She'd kept up with him when Davey was a baby but as the boy grew into a toddler, he liked notice if things were going to change. Henry had never been willing to accept the difficulty of swooping in and changing Davey's schedule without warning. Davey's difficulty with change only got worse over time, and it had become a huge source of tension with Henry.

Since returning to Crimson, Emily had done her best

to keep her son on a regular schedule. Her mother and Noah had quickly adapted, making her understand the issues her ex-husband had were his own and not her or Davey's fault.

She filled a plastic cup with milk for Davey, then pulled out two beers for her and Jase. As she was setting the table, Jase let himself back into the house. "Perfect dogs," he said, holding up a plate.

"Do you know Tater?"

Emily turned to find Davey standing behind her, looking at Jase.

"She's my uncle Noah's dog," the boy explained. "Her fur is really soft, but she has stinky breath and she likes to lick me."

"Tater is a great dog," Jase answered, setting the hot dogs on the kitchen table.

"Let's wash hands," she said to her son. "Mac and cheese and hot dogs for dinner."

He climbed on the stool in front of the sink, washed his hands, then went to sit next to Jase at the table. "Tater used to live here with Uncle Noah. Now they both live with Aunt Katie. Do you have a dog?"

Jase nodded. "I have a puppy. Her name is Ruby."

"Does she have soft fur?"

"She sure does and I bet she'd like you. She's six months old and has lots of energy. She loves to play."

"I could play with her," Davey offered, taking a big bite of mac and cheese.

"Would you like to meet her sometime?"

Davey nodded. "We can drive to where you live after dinner."

"If that's okay with your mom," Jase told him.

"A short visit," Emily said, trying not to make Davey's

suggestion into something bigger than it was. Which was difficult, because her son never volunteered to go anywhere. She planned outings to local parks and different shops downtown, and Davey tolerated the excursions. But there was no place he'd ever asked to go. Until now. She wondered if Jase understood the significance of the request.

He tipped back his beer bottle for a drink and then smiled at her. "I love mac and cheese."

She rolled her eyes but Davey nodded. "Me, too. And hot dogs. Mommy makes good cheese quesadillas."

"I'll have to try for an invitation to quesadilla night."

"You can come to dinner again." Davey kept his gaze on his plate, the words tumbling out of his mouth with little inflection. "Right, Mommy?"

"Of course," she whispered.

Jase asked Davey a question about his latest Lego creation. Once again, her son was talking more with Jase than he normally would to his family. Henry had a habit of demanding Davey make eye contact and enunciate when he spoke, both of which were difficult for her quiet boy. The last six months of her marriage had been fraught with tension as she and her ex-husband had waged a devastating battle over how to raise their son. The arguments and tirades had made Davey shrink into himself even more, and she'd worried the damage Henry was unwittingly doing might leave permanent scars on Davey's sensitive personality.

The way he acted toward Jase was a revelation. When Jase smiled at her again, his eyes warm and tender, Emily's heart began to race. How could she resist this man who saw her at her worst—angry or in the middle of an emotional meltdown—and still remained at her side, constant and true?

The answer was she didn't want to fight the spark between them. For the first time since returning to Crimson, Emily wondered if she hadn't squandered her chance at happiness after all.

"She needs to go out and do her business, and then you can play with her." Jase unlocked the front door of his house as he spoke to Davey.

The young boy stayed behind Emily's legs but nodded.

Emily gave him an apologetic smile. "He always takes a few minutes to acclimate to new places."

"Take all the time you need, buddy." As soon as the door began to open, Ruby started yelping. "She's usually pretty excited when I first get home."

"Davey, let's go," Emily said, her voice tense.

Jase looked over his shoulder to see the boy still standing in front of the door, eyes on the floor of the porch.

She crouched down next to her son. "It's okay, sweetie. You wanted to meet the puppy. Remember?"

"Take your time," Jase called. "I'm going to bring her to the backyard because it's fenced. Come on out whenever you're ready." The yelping got more insistent, a sure sign Ruby needed to get to the grass quickly. He lifted the blanket off the crate in the corner and flipped open the door, grabbing the puppy in his arms as she tried to dart out. She wriggled in his arms and licked his chin, but as soon as he opened the back door she darted for her favorite potty spot near a tree in the corner. He followed her into the grass with a glance back to the house. Emily and Davey hadn't emerged yet.

Ruby ran back to him and head-butted his shin before circling his legs. He didn't bother to hide his smile. Even after the worst day, it was hard not to feel better as the recipient of so much unconditional love. It didn't matter how long he'd been gone. She greeted him with off-the-charts enthusiasm every time.

After a few minutes, Ruby stopped, her whole body going rigid as her focus shifted to the back of the house. Jase went to grab her but she dodged his grasp and took off for the porch. He called for her but she ignored him as a six-month-old puppy was apt to do.

To his surprise, she slowed down at the top of the patio steps and didn't bark once at Emily or Davey. His puppy normally gave a vocal greeting at every new person or animal she encountered. She trotted toward Emily, stopping long enough to be petted before moving closer to Davey.

The boy was standing ramrod stiff against the house's brick exterior, his gaze staring straight ahead. Jase could almost feel Emily holding her breath. Ruby sniffed at Davey's legs, then nudged his fingers with her nose. When he didn't pet her, she bumped him again, then sat a few feet in front of him as if content to wait. After a moment, Davey's chin dipped and he glanced at the puppy. She rewarded him by prancing in a circle, then sitting again. He slowly eased himself away from the house and took a hesitant step toward her.

Ruby whined softly and ran to the edge of the porch and returned to Davey with a tennis ball in her mouth, dropping it at his feet. The ball rolled a few inches.

"She's learning to play fetch," Jase called. "Do you want to throw the ball for her?"

Davey didn't give any indication he'd heard the question other than picking up the ball gingerly between his fingers and tossing it down the steps. Ruby tumbled after it, and in her excitement to retrieve the ball, she lost her balance and did a somersault across the grass. With a small laugh, Davey made his way down the steps toward the grass.

Ruby returned the ball to him and the boy threw it again.

"She'll go after the ball all night long," he told the boy. "Let me know when you get tired of throwing it."

Davey walked farther into the yard.

Jase turned for the patio to find Emily standing on the top step, tears shining in her blue eyes. "What's wrong?" he asked, jogging up the stairs to her side.

She shook her head. "Davey laughed. Did you hear him laugh?"

"Puppies have that effect on people."

"I can't remember the last time he laughed out loud," she whispered, swiping under her eyes. "It's the most beautiful sound."

"I'm glad I got to hear it."

Ruby flipped over again as she dived for the ball and this time when Davey giggled, Emily let out her own quiet laugh. She clapped a hand over her mouth.

Jase wrapped an arm around her shoulder. "It's been a while since I've heard his mother laugh, too."

"I don't know whether to laugh or cry." She sank down to the top step and Jase followed, his heart expanding as she leaned against him. "He used to laugh when he was a baby. Then things went sideways... He became so disconnected."

"You're a good mom, Em. You'll get him through this."

She turned to look at him. "Do you really believe that? You don't think I messed him up by leaving Henry and moving him across the country?"

"You protected him. That's what a mom is supposed to do." He tried not to let decades-old bitterness creep into his voice but must have failed because Emily laced her fingers with his.

"How old were you when your mother left town?"

"Nine. My sister was seven. I haven't seen either of them since the day Mom packed up the car and drove away."

"Have you ever looked?"

"My mother made it clear any man with the last name Crenshaw was bound for trouble."

"She was wrong. You've changed what people in this town think of your family. She needs to know who you've become."

"It's too late."

"What about your sister?"

"I don't blame her. Who knows how my mother poisoned her against my dad and me. I'm sure Sierra has a good life. She doesn't need me."

Emily squeezed his hand. "I didn't think I needed my family when I left Crimson. I was stupid."

He glanced down at their entwined fingers and ran his thumb along the half-moons of her nails. "You used to wear polish."

"You're changing the subject." She waved to Davey

with her free hand when he turned. The boy gave her a slight nod and went back to throwing the ball.

"I don't want to talk about my family tonight." He threw her a sideways glance. "My turn for a pass?"

"Fine. Let's go back to my former beauty routine, which is a fascinating topic. I had my signature nail color and perfume. I was determined to be someone people remembered."

"You were."

"For the wrong reasons," she said with a laugh. "It's pretty sad if the thing I'm recognized for is a top-notch manicure and a cloud of expensive perfume."

"Now they'll recognize you as a strong woman and an amazing mother." He leaned closer to her until his nose touched the soft skin of her neck. "Although you still smell good."

Her breath hitched. "I wish I hadn't been so mean to you when we were younger."

"I suppose you'll have to make it up to me."

She turned, and he was unnerved by her serious expression. "I'm not the right woman for you, Jase."

The certainty of her tone made his gut clench. "Shouldn't I be the one making that decision?"

"I'm doing you a favor by making it for you."

"I don't want favors from you." He narrowed his eyes. "Unless they involve your mouth on me. Isn't that what you told me you wanted?"

Color rose to her cheeks and she dropped her gaze. "Wanting and needing are two different things."

He *wanted* to haul her into his lap and kiss that lie off her mouth. It was becoming more difficult to be patient when she was sitting so close that the warmth of her thigh seeped into his skin.

"We should talk about plans for the prewedding parties." She tugged her fingers out his and inched away from him until the cool evening breeze whispered in the space between their bodies. Jase hated that space. "Since so many of Noah's and Katie's friends overlap, I think the bachelorette and bachelor parties should be combined."

"Makes sense. Party planning is not exactly my strong suit."

"You're lucky I'm here."

There were many more reasons, but she was already spooked, so he didn't mention any of them. "I can tell you have an idea."

She flashed him a superior grin. "A scavenger hunt."

"Like we did as kids?"

"Sort of. We'll put together groups and give everyone clues to search for items important to Noah and Katie. They both grew up here so there's plenty of things to choose from."

"I like it," Jase admitted.

"Because it's brilliant."

"That's the Emily I know and…" He paused, watched her eyes widen, then added, "like as a friend."

She bumped him with her shoulder. "Mr. Perfect and a comedian—quite a combination."

"We've already established I'm not perfect."

"I like you better as a real person." She nudged him again. "And a friend."

As the sun began to fade, they watched Davey throw the ball over and over to the puppy.

"I wonder who will give up first," Jase muttered. The answer came a few minutes later when Ruby dropped the ball on the grass in front of Davey, then flopped down next to it.

"Wavy-Davey, it's time to head home," Emily called to him. "Bedtime for puppies and little boys."

The boy ignored her and sat next to Ruby, buried his face in the puppy's fur and began to gently rock back and forth.

Emily sighed. "Too much stimulation," she said, a sudden weariness in her eyes. "You might want to go inside. Chances are likely he'll have a tantrum."

"How do you know?"

"The rocking is one of his tells." She pressed her hand to her forehead. "I should have monitored him more closely but…" She gave Jase a watery smile. "I was having fun."

"Me, too," he told her and lifted his fingers to the back of her neck, massaging gently. "I'm not going to leave you. He's a kid and if he has a tantrum, so be it."

"I don't want the night to end like this." She walked down the steps slowly, approaching her son the way she might a wounded animal. Jase followed a few paces behind.

"Davey, we're going back to Grandma's now."

The rocking became more vigorous.

"Do you want to walk to the car or should I carry you?"

"No."

"You can decide or I'll decide for you, sweetheart." Emily's tone was gentle but firm. "Either way we're going home. You can visit Ruby again."

Davey's movement slowed. "When?"

"Maybe this weekend."

He shook his head and Jase stepped forward. "Hey,

buddy, you did an awesome job tiring out Ruby. I bet she's going to sleep the whole night through."

"She likes the ball," the boy mumbled.

"She likes you throwing the ball," Jase told him. "But even as tired as she is, I bet she'll wake up tomorrow morning with a ton of energy."

Davey gave him a short nod.

"Do you think it would be okay if I brought her out to your grandma's farm in the morning? You can puppy-sit while I go to a meeting."

The boy glanced up at him, then back at Ruby. He nodded again.

Jase crouched down next to Davey. "I'll ask your mom if it's okay with her, but you have to get a good night's sleep, too. That means heading home now and going to bed without a fuss. Do you think you can do that?"

Davey got to his feet and lifted his face to look at Emily before lowering his gaze again. "Can Ruby come over in the morning, Mommy?"

Emily reached out as if to ruffle her son's hair, then pulled her hand tight to her chest. "You'll have to eat breakfast early."

"Okay."

"Then it's fine with me. Your grammy will love to meet Ruby."

"She can walk with us." Without another word, he turned for the house. "Let's go home, Mommy."

Jase bent and scooped the sleeping puppy into his arms. Ruby snuggled against him.

Emily ran her hand through the dog's fur, then cupped Jase's cheek. "Thank you," she whispered and pressed a soft kiss to his mouth.

"A better way to end the night?" he asked against her lips.

"Much better. Good luck at the breakfast tomorrow." She kissed him again, then ran up the back steps.

Jase followed with the dog in his arms, watching as Emily buckled her son into his booster seat. He waved to Davey as they drove away.

"You did good," he whispered to the puppy sleeping in his arms and walked back to his house.

Chapter Eight

"You're looking at those pancakes like they're topped with motor oil instead of syrup."

Emily smiled as Jase spun toward her, almost spilling his cup of coffee in the process.

"You came," he said.

She glanced around at the basement reception room of one of Crimson's oldest churches. The last time she'd been here was after her father's funeral, but she tried to ignore the memories that seemed to bounce from the walls. Instead she waved a hand at the display of Sunday school artwork. "Where else would I be on a beautiful Saturday morning?"

"I don't really need to answer that, do I?"

"No, but I would like to know why the candidate who sponsored this breakfast is hiding out in the corner? Are you familiar with the term *glad-handing*?"

"I'm eating breakfast," he mumbled, pointing to the paper plate stacked with pancakes that sat on the small folding table shoved against the wall. "They're actually quite good." He set down his coffee cup and picked up the plate, lifting a forkful of pancake toward her mouth.

"I had oatmeal earlier."

"Edna Sharpe is watching. You don't want her to think you're too good for her pancakes."

Emily rolled her eyes at the glint of challenge in his gaze. But she allowed him to feed her a bite. "Yum," she murmured as she chewed. Her breath caught as Jase used his thumb to wipe a drop of syrup from the corner of her mouth.

"Jase," she whispered, "why aren't you talking to everyone?"

He dropped the plate back to the table and folded his arms across his chest. "I hate how they look at me."

"Like you're Crimson's favorite son?"

"Like I'm the poor, pathetic kid with the mother who abandoned him to his drunken dad." He held up a hand when she started to speak. "I understand most people in town know my family's history. But I've worked hard to make sure they see me and not the Crenshaw legacy. Now Charles Thompson is leaking small details about my childhood—dirty laundry I don't want aired—to anyone who will listen. You know how fast those bits of information travel through the town grapevine."

"So you're going to let him have the last word? Give up on everything you've done for Crimson?"

"Of course not."

She pointed toward the crowded tables. "Then go visit with these people. Shake hands. Kiss babies."

"Kiss babies," he repeated, one side of his mouth curving. "Really?"

"You know what I mean. I understand what happens when you let someone else's perceived image guide your actions. That's not who you are."

"They expect—"

"You're not perfect. Neither is your history. People can deal with that. But you have to put yourself out there."

"Is that what you're doing?"

"I'm supporting a friend," she said and straightened his tie.

His warm hands covered hers. "I'm glad you're here, Em. I could use a friend right now."

"What you could use is a kick in the pants."

His smile widened. "Are you offering to be the kicker?"

She nodded. "Katie and Noah are stopping by in a bit and I left a message for Natalie."

"You didn't need to. It's a Saturday morning and they have lives."

"Support goes both ways, and you've given plenty to your friends. They're happy to return the favor."

He took a deep, shuddering breath. "There wasn't supposed to be this much scrutiny."

"Welcome to the joys of a political campaign."

"And part of a life you left behind." He bent his knees until they were at eye level. "This isn't the plan for rebuilding your life." His fingers brushed a strand of hair away from her face. A flicker of longing skittered across her skin, one that was becoming all too familiar with this man.

"I can help," she said with a shrug. "It's what I know how to do."

He glanced over her shoulder and cursed. "My father is here," he said on a harsh breath.

Emily could feel the change in Jase, the walls shooting up around him. "You mingle with the voters," she said quickly. "I'll talk to your dad."

"You don't have to—"

"Too late," she called over her shoulder. She hurried to the entrance of the reception hall, where Jase's father stood by himself. A few of the groups at tables nearby threw him questioning looks. Emily knew Declan Crenshaw's history as well as anyone. The man had been on and off the wagon more times than anyone could count.

Once Jase and Noah had become friends, Emily's whole family had been pulled into the strange orbit circling Declan and his demons. Jase had slept over at her parents' farm most weekends, and she remembered several times being woken in the dead of night to Declan standing in their front yard, screaming for Jase to come home and make him something to eat.

As a stupid, spoiled teenage girl, Emily had hated being associated with the town drunk. She'd unfairly taken her resentment out on Jase, treating him like he was beneath her. Shame at the memory rose like bile in her throat. She'd been such a fool.

Now Declan's gaze flicked to her, wary and unsure behind the fake smile he'd plastered across his face. Without hesitating, Emily wrapped him in a tight hug.

"Jase is so glad you could make it," she said, loud enough so the people sitting nearby were sure to hear.

"You're a beautiful liar," Declan murmured in her ear, "and I know you hate these events as much as I do."

She pulled back, adjusted the collar on his worn dress shirt much as she'd straightened his son's tie. Declan would have been a distinguished man if the years hadn't been so hard on him. "Maybe not quite as much. I wasn't very nice, but at least I never embarrassed the people who loved me."

"Good point," he admitted with a frown, his shaggy eyebrows pulling low. "But things are different now. I'm sober for good. Am I ever going to live down the past?"

"I'm more concerned Jase feels the need to live it down for you." She led him toward the line at the pancake table.

"I know what Charles Thompson is trying to do." Declan picked up a paper plate and stabbed a stack of pancakes with a plastic fork. "It's my fault and it's not fair."

"Life rarely is." Emily took one pancake for herself. "We both know that."

"You're good for him."

She shook her head. "I'm not. As small of a community as Crimson is, the life Jase has here is still more public than I'm willing to handle."

Declan greeted the older man standing behind the table wiping a bottle of syrup. "Morning, Phil."

The other man's eyes narrowed. "Surprised to see you out of bed so early, Crenshaw."

Emily braced herself for Declan's retort, but he only smiled. "I'm full of surprises. How are Margie and the kids?"

Phil blinked several times before clearing his throat. "They're fine."

"I heard you have a grandbaby on the way." Declan poured syrup over his pancakes.

DO YOU WANT TO GET REWARDED WITH FREE BOOKS?

HARLEQUIN® My Rewards

Join today.
It's fun, easy, and free...

REWARD THE BOOK LOVER IN YOU WITH HARLEQUIN MY REWARDS

Here's How It Works:

Earn FREE BOOKS Join Today! HarlequinMyRewards.com

Sign Up!
It's free and easy to join!
Register at **www.harlequinmyrewards.com**

Start Earning Points!
Get 2000 points** right
now just for signing up.

Claim your Rewards!
Get FREE BOOKS, GIFTS and MORE!

Join today and get a FREE Book!
HarlequinMyRewards.com

**Offer ends 09/31/16

"My daughter-in-law is due around Thanksgiving," the other man answered, his face relaxing.

"I can't wait for Jase to find the right girl," Declan said. He nudged Emily's plate with his, which she ignored. "But until then, he's giving everything he has to this town. Do you know how many times he's taken payment for his services as a lawyer with casseroles or muffins?"

"I don't," Phil admitted. Several other volunteers had gathered around him.

Declan leaned over the table and lowered his voice, as if he was imparting a great secret. "More than I can count. He shares the food with me, and while I appreciate it, blueberry muffins don't pay the bills. But Jase wants to help people. There's his work on city council and getting Liam Donovan to move his company headquarters here." Declan glanced toward the doors leading into the hall. "There's Liam now, along with Noah Crawford. My son is good for this town, you know?"

The group on the other side of the table nodded in unison. "We know," Phil said.

With a satisfied nod, Declan turned to Emily, his dark eyes sparkling. "Shall we sit down and have breakfast, darlin'?"

She nodded, stunned, and followed him to a table, waving Noah and Liam over toward them. "You were amazing."

He threw back his head and laughed. "That's the first time I've ever heard that adjective used to describe me."

"I thought you'd get angry when Phil made the comment about you getting out of bed early."

"I don't get mad about hearing the truth. Phil and I go way back. It may have taken me a whole morning to climb out of bed in my hangover days, but at least I wasn't wearing my wife's undies when I did."

Emily felt her mouth drop. "What are you talking about?" she asked in a hushed whisper.

He winked at her. "I know plenty about the people in this town. For years, there was only one bar the locals liked. My butt was glued to one of the vinyl stools more nights than I care to admit. Most folks like to talk and they figure a drunk isn't going to remember their secrets." He tapped the side of his head with one finger. "But I got a mind like a steel trap. Even three sheets to the wind, I don't forget what I hear."

"There's more to you than anyone knows," Emily murmured with a small smile. She wouldn't forget what this man had put Jase through because of his drunken antics, but she could tell Declan was sincere in his desire to support his son.

"I think we have that in common," Declan told her.

A moment later Noah put an arm around her shoulder. "Hey there, sis. Trading one politician for another?"

She shoved him away, panic slicing up her spine.

"I'm joking, Em," Noah said quickly. "Didn't mean to strike a nerve."

"You should let Katie do the talking while you stick to looking the part of a handsome forest ranger." Emily tried to play off her reaction, but the way Noah watched her said he wasn't fooled.

He smiled anyway, smoothing a hand over his uniform. "I *am* a handsome forest ranger." His expression sobered as he looked over her shoulder. "Hello, Mr. Crenshaw."

"Noah." Declan nodded. "Congratulations on your upcoming wedding."

"Thanks. I owe a debt of thanks to Jase for helping me realize the love of my life had been by my side for years." He moved back a step to include Liam in the conversation. "Have you met Liam Donovan?"

Declan stuck out his hand. "I haven't but I've heard you're rich enough to buy the whole damn mountain if you wanted it."

Noah looked mortified but Liam only smiled and shook Declan's hand. "Maybe half the mountain," he answered.

As she greeted Liam, Emily could feel her brother studying her. She and Noah hadn't been close after their father's death, especially since they'd each been wrestling with their own private grief, and neither very successfully. They'd begun to forge a new bond since returning to Crimson, but Emily wasn't ready to hear his thoughts on her being a part of Jase's life.

Pushing back from the table, she grabbed her plate and stood. "You two keep Declan company. I see an old high school friend." She leaned down to give Jase's father a quick hug. "Thanks for breakfast," she said with a wink.

"Best date I've had in years."

Noah looked like he wanted to stop her, but she ducked around him and headed for the trash can in the corner. She waved to a couple of her mother's friends, then searched for Jase amid the people mingling at the sides of the reception hall.

Of course he was in the middle of the largest group, gesturing as he spoke and making eye contact with each person. They all stood riveted by whatever he was saying, nodding and offering up encouraging smiles.

A momentary flash of jealousy stabbed at her heart.

She understood what it was like to be on the receiving end of Jase's attention, sincere and unguarded. He was the only man she knew who could make his gaze feel like a caress against her skin, and this morning was proof of why that was so dangerous to her.

Even when he was living up to other peoples' expectations, Jase was comfortable in the role. He belonged in the spotlight and in the hearts of this town. Emily had left behind her willingness to trade her private life for public favor. Davey had changed her. She'd never put anyone else's needs before his. Even her own.

She slipped out the door leading to the back of the church, needing a moment away from the curious eyes of the town. The midmorning sun was warm on her skin. She closed her eyes and tipped up her face, leaning back against the building's brick wall.

A moment later the door opened and shut again.

"What happened to catching up with old friends?" Noah asked, coming to stand in front of her.

"You're blocking my sun," she told him.

"Because from what I remember of how you left this town, you don't have many friends here."

She opened her eyes to glare at him. "Don't be mean."

He sighed. "I don't understand what you're doing. For years you couldn't stand Jase—"

"That's not true." The protest sounded weak even to her own ears.

"You certainly gave him a hard time. I stopped out at the farm this morning and saw Mom and Davey with his puppy."

"Davey bonded with Ruby right away, so Jase was nice enough to bring her by so they could play."

"Of course. Jase is a nice guy."

"Too nice for someone like me?"

Noah stepped out of her line of sight, turning so he stood next to her against the wall. "You know he's had a crush on you for years."

"It's different now. I'm working for him."

"Which means you two are spending a lot of time together. He'd moved on until you came back. Jase has a lot of responsibility in this town. Between his practice, his father and now dealing with a real campaign—"

"I understand, Noah." She hated being put on the spot and the fact her brother was doing it. "Are you telling me to stay away from him?"

Noah shook his head. "You're coming off a bad divorce. I'm saying don't use Jase as a rebound fling. Both of you could end up hurt."

Pushing off the wall, she spun toward him. "It's Jase you're worried about, not me."

"Emily—"

"No. You don't know anything about my marriage."

"Why is that?" He ran a hand through his hair. "How the hell am I supposed to understand anything about your life? You cut me out after Dad died."

"That was mutual and you know it."

"I thought we were doing better since Mom's illness?"

"We are, Noah. But it might be too soon for brotherly lectures on my private life."

"Nothing is private in Crimson. You know that. Besides, I thought you came back to here to heal?"

"Maybe Jase is a part of me healing." Until she said the words out loud, she hadn't realized how true they were. Tears sprang to the backs of her eyes and she swiped at her cheek, refusing to allow herself to break down. She'd promised herself she was finished with crying after she'd left Henry.

Noah cursed under his breath. "I'm sorry. Don't cry."

"I'm not crying," she whispered and her voice cracked.

"You really care about him."

"We're friends. It's not a fling. Not a rebound. I don't know what is going on between us, but I'm not going to hurt him. I think…" She paused, forced herself to meet Noah's worried gaze. "I think I'm good for him. It goes both ways, Noah. I know it does."

"Okay, honey." Noah pulled her in for a tight hug. She resisted at first, holding on to her anger like an old friend. But her brother didn't let go, and after a few moments she sagged against him, understanding that even if he made her crazy, Noah was far better comfort than her temper could ever be.

"I'm sorry," he whispered into her hair.

"You're a good friend to Jase."

"But I need to be a better brother to you. You're important to me. You and Davey both."

"You have to say that because I helped your bride pick out a wedding dress that will bring tears to your eyes."

"I can't wait," he said with a lopsided grin and a dopey look in his eyes that made her smile. "But I'm *choosing* to tell you the truth about supporting you more. I mean every word."

"Then will you help me find my own place to live?"

"Mom loves having you at the farm." He frowned. "She loves helping with Davey and having you close."

"I'll still be close, but I want a home of my own, even

if it's a tiny apartment somewhere. After the wedding will you help me look?"

"Of course."

"Do you have any prewedding nerves?" she asked, stepping out of his embrace. "You spent a long time avoiding commitment."

"I was a master," he agreed.

"Marriage is a big deal, especially when there's a baby on the way."

"I felt the baby kick the other night."

"Oh, Noah."

"It made this whole thing feel real. I mean, I know it's real but…yes, I'm nervous." He looked over her shoulder toward the mountains in the distance. "Not about marrying Katie. I can't believe I was blind for so long, but now I've got her and I'm never letting go." He took a breath, then said, "Even if I don't deserve her."

"You do." She nudged him with her hip. "You're a pain in my butt, but you deserve happiness."

"What if I mess up? What if I can't be as good as Dad?"

"Don't compare yourself." She gave a small laugh. "Do you think I could ever hold a candle to Mom?"

"You're an amazing mother."

"You'll be an amazing dad." She held up her hand, fist closed. "We've got this, bro."

"Are you trying to be cool?"

She shrugged and lifted her hand higher. "Don't leave me hanging."

With a laugh, Noah fist-bumped her, then pulled her in for another hug. "We'd better head back inside. I have a feeling Declan and Liam together are a dangerous combination."

* * *

Jase's lungs burned as he ran the final stretch to the lookout point halfway up the main Crimson Mountain trail. At the top, he bent forward, sucking in the thin mountain air.

The late-afternoon trail run was supposed to clear his head, but his mind refused to slow down. Images of Emily and his dad swirled inside him, mixing with thoughts of the questions he'd answered at this morning's campaign breakfast.

How do you feel about Charles Thompson running against you?

Do you have too much going on to add mayor to your list of responsibilities?

When are you going to settle down and start a family?

Are you worried about not having time to take care of your dad?

What if Declan starts to drink again?

He'd answered each of the inquiries with a nod and an understanding smile, but he'd wanted to turn and run from the crowded church hall. Those questions brought up too many emotions inside him. Too much turmoil he couldn't control. Jase's greatest fear was losing control and it seemed he had less of a grasp on it with each passing day.

He sank down to one of the rock formations and watched as Liam Donovan came over the final ridge, a few minutes behind Jase. Liam's dark hair was stuck to his forehead and his athletic T-shirt plastered to his chest. The run up to the lookout point was almost three miles of vertical switchbacks. Jase had been running this trail since high school but today even the beauty of the forest hadn't settled him.

"Are you crazy?" Liam asked, panting even harder than Jase. "You were running like a mountain lion was chasing you."

Jase wiped the back of one arm across his forehead. "A mountain lion would have caught you instead of me. I thought you wanted a challenge."

"A challenge is different than a heart attack. You'd have a tough time explaining to Natalie that you left me on the side of the mountain."

"I wouldn't have left you." Jase grinned. "I'm too afraid of your wife."

"The strange thing is she'd take that as a compliment." He sat on a rock across from Jase. "You had a good turnout at the breakfast this morning."

"I appreciate you stopping by."

"Always happy to do my part with a plate of pancakes. Your dad is a character."

Jase laughed. "That's one word for him."

"He's really proud of you." Liam used the hem of his shirt to wipe the sweat off his face. "My dad never gave a damn about anything I did. Not as long as I stayed out of his way."

Liam's father owned one of the most successful tech companies in the world. It had been big news in the technology world when Liam broke off to start his own GPS software company and chose Crimson as the headquarters for it.

"I couldn't exactly stay out of Declan's way. I was too busy cleaning up behind him."

"A fact your new opponent in the mayor's race is exploiting?"

Jase blew out a breath. "Sheriff Thompson has seen me at my lowest. He and my dad grew up together in town and the Thompsons and Crenshaws have always been rivals—sports, women, you name it." He stood and paced to the edge of the ridge, taking in the view of the town below. "Anytime a situation involved my dad, Thompson made sure he was on the scene. Didn't matter if it was the weekend or who was on duty. The sheriff always showed up to personally cuff Dad."

"Declan seems sincere about changing."

"He's always sincere." From up here, Jase could see downtown Crimson and the neighborhoods fanning out around it. The creek ran along the edge of downtown, then meandered through the valley and into the thick forest on the other side.

As a kid, he'd battled the expectations that he'd follow in his father's footsteps. People always seemed to be waiting for him to make a misstep, to become another casualty of the Crenshaw legend. He'd worked so hard to prove them wrong. When would he be released from the responsibility of making up for mistakes he hadn't made?

Liam came to stand next to him. "I know what it's like to have to claw your way out from a father's shadow. Our backgrounds are different, but disappointment and anger don't discriminate based on how much you have in the bank."

"But you've escaped it."

"Maybe," Liam said with a shrug. "Maybe not. My dad is known all over the world. I've created a different future for myself but his legacy follows me. I choose to ignore it and live life on my terms."

Jase wasn't sure if he'd even know how to go about

setting up his own life away from the restrictions of his past. "When I graduated from law school, a firm in Denver offered me a position. I turned it down to come back to Crimson and take over Andrew Meyer's family practice."

"Do you regret the choice you made?"

Jase picked up a flat stone from the trail and hurled it over the edge of the ridge. It arced out, then disappeared into the canopy of trees below. "I don't know. Back then, I was so determined to return to Crimson as a success. Part of it was feeling like I owed something to the people in this town. As much as they judged my family, they also came forward to take care of us when things were rough. After my mom left, we had food in the freezer for months."

"Nothing says love in a small town like a casserole."

"Exactly," Jase agreed with a laugh. "There were a couple of teachers who looked after me at school. Once it became clear I was determined to stay on the straight and narrow, the town was generous with its support. I was given a partial scholarship during undergrad and always had a job waiting for me in the summer. I wanted to pay back that kindness, and dedicating myself to the town seemed like the best way to do it."

"But…" Liam prompted.

"I've started to wonder what it would have been like to go to work, come home and take care of only myself. Maybe that's selfish—"

"It's not selfish." Liam lobbed a rock over the side and it followed the same trajectory as Jase's. "It's also not too late. I was going to ask if you need support with the campaign. Financial support," he clarified.

"But now I'm wondering if becoming mayor is what you really want?"

"Does it matter? I've committed to it."

"You can back out. Charles Thompson isn't a bad man. He would do a decent job."

Jase cocked a brow.

"Not as good as you, of course. But the future of Crimson doesn't rest on your shoulders, Jase."

"I'll think about that." As if he could think about anything else. "We should head back down. I'll take it easy on you."

Liam barked out a laugh. "A true gentleman."

Jase started for the trail, then turned back. "Thanks for the offer, Liam. I appreciate it, but I don't want to owe you. Having you at my back is plenty of support."

"I'd think of it as an investment," Liam answered. "And the offer stands if you change your mind."

"Thank you." Jase started running, the descent more technical than climbing the switchbacks due to the loose rocks and late-afternoon shadows falling over the trail. It was just what he needed, something to concentrate on besides the emotional twists and turns of his current life.

Chapter Nine

Monday morning, Emily jumped at the tap on her shoulder, spinning around in her desk chair to find Jase grinning at her.

She ripped the headphones off her ears. "You scared me half to death," she said, wheezing in a breath.

"You were singing out loud."

"You were supposed to be in court all day." She narrowed her eyes.

"What exactly are you listening to?" He reached for the headphones, but she grabbed them, then spun around to hit the mute button on her keyboard.

"Music," she mumbled. "Why are you back so early? I didn't hear the bells on the door when it opened."

"I came in through the door to the alley out back."

"You snuck up on me," she grumbled.

"What kind of music? I didn't recognize it."

"Broadway show tunes, okay?" She crossed her arms over her chest and glared. "*Evita* to be specific. I like musicals." The words came out like a challenge. "You're a lawyer—sue me."

His grin widened. "Don't cry for me, Emily Whitaker."

"Asking for trouble, Jase Crenshaw."

He held up a brown paper bag. "Here's a peace offering. I brought lunch from the deli around the corner. That's why I came through the back. Have you eaten?"

She held up an empty granola-bar wrapper. "I'm working through lunch since I'm leaving early today." Tomorrow was Davey's first day of kindergarten so tonight they were going to the ice cream social at the elementary school. Her son didn't seem worried about the change, but Emily had been a bundle of nerves since the moment she'd woken up this morning.

She'd had a meeting at the beginning of the week with the kindergarten teacher and the school's interventionist to discuss the Asperger's and how to help Davey have a successful school year. For a small school district, Crimson Elementary School offered many special education services. This would mark the first time he'd been away from her during the day.

She'd enrolled him in preschool in their Boston neighborhood, having added Davey's name to the exclusive program's wait list when he was only a few months old. Despite the expense of the private program, the teachers had been unwilling to work with his personality quirks.

Much like her husband, they'd expected him to manage like the rest of the children, which led to several frustrated tantrums. Davey had lashed out, throwing a toy car across the room. It had hit one of the other students on the side of the head and the girl had stumbled, then fallen, knocking her head on the corner of a bookshelf. There'd been angry calls from both the teacher and the girl's mother and even a parent meeting at the school to allay other families' concerns about Davey continuing in the program.

Henry had been furious, mostly because two of his partners had kids enrolled at the school so he couldn't brush the incident under the rug. In the end, Emily had pulled Davey, opting to work with him herself on the skills he'd needed to be ready for kindergarten.

She couldn't control the way Asperger's affected his personality and his ability to socialize with both adults and other kids. Or how he was treated by people who didn't understand how special he was.

"Come to the conference room and eat a real lunch," Jase said gently, as if he could sense the anxiety tumbling through her like rocks skidding down the side of Crimson Mountain.

"I have work to do."

"Em, you are the most efficient person I've ever met. You've already organized this whole office, updated the billing system, caught up on all my outstanding correspondence and done such a great job of editing the briefs that Judge McIlwain at the courthouse actually commented on it."

Pride, unfamiliar and precious, bloomed in her chest. "He did?"

"Yes, and he's not the only one." Jase rested his hip against the corner of her desk. "Do you remember the contract you drafted for the firm I'm working with over in Aspen?"

She nodded.

"The office manager called to see if I'd used a service to hire my new assistant. She wanted to find someone just like you for their senior partner. He's a stickler for detail and notoriously hard on office staff."

"She called me, too." Emily swallowed.

"Why?" Jase's tone was suspiciously even.

"To offer me a job."

"What was the starting salary?"

She told him the number, almost double what he was paying her.

Jase cursed under his breath. "Why didn't you take it? It's one of the most prestigious firms in the state."

"I know. I researched them."

"They can offer you benefits and an actual career path. You have to consider it, even if it makes me mad as hell hearing someone tried to poach you."

She shook her head. "I don't want to work in Aspen. I like it here with you." She flashed what she hoped was a teasing smile. "You'd be lost without me."

His brown eyes were serious when he replied, "You have no idea."

"Jase…"

"At least let me feed you. I've been thinking of ideas for the prewedding scavenger hunt."

She stood at the same time he did, too shocked to protest any longer. "You have?"

He looked confused. "Wasn't that the plan?"

"Well, yes," she admitted as she followed him to the conference room at the far end of the hall. "But I wasn't sure you'd take it seriously. You have so much going on, and it's a silly party theme."

There was an ancient table in the middle of the conference room, with eight chairs surrounding it. On her second day in the office, Emily had taken wood soap and furniture wax to the dull surface, polishing it until it gleamed a rich mahogany. She liked that she could make a difference here in Jase's small law practice.

He held out a chair for her and she sat, watching as he emptied the contents of the bag. He set a wax-paper-wrapped sandwich in front of her, along with a bag of barbecue potato chips. "Noah is my best friend. Making his wedding weekend special isn't silly, and neither was your idea. You need to give yourself more credit."

She nodded but didn't meet his gaze, running one finger over the seam of the wax paper. "What kind of sandwich?"

"Turkey and avocado on wheat," he answered absently. "Do you want a soda?"

"Diet, please," she said, unable to take her hand off the sandwich.

He left the room and Emily sucked in a breath. He remembered her favorite sandwich.

The small gesture leveled her, and the barriers she'd placed around her heart collapsed. This man who was wrong for her in every way except the one that mattered. He seemed to want her just the way she was. Her ex-husband would have brought her a salad, forever concerned she might not remain a perfect size six.

Perfect.

Her life since returning to her hometown had been anything but perfect, yet she wouldn't trade the journey that had brought her here. She was a better person for her independence and the effort she'd put into protecting Davey from any more suffering and rejection.

* * *

She did her best to gather her strength as she pulled up to the elementary school parking lot later that evening. The playground and grassy field in front of the building were crowded with people, and she wished she'd gotten to the event earlier.

Instead she'd changed clothes several times before she and Davey left her mother's house. Difficult to find an outfit that conveyed all the things she needed.

I'm a good mother. Like me. Like my son. Accept us here so I can make it a true home.

Straightening her simple A-line skirt, she got out of the SUV and helped Davey hop down from his booster seat. The desire to gather him close almost overwhelmed her. She wanted to ground herself to him with touch but knew that would only make him anxious. She dropped the car keys into her purse and gave him a bright smile. "Are you ready to meet your new teacher?"

His eyes shifted to hers, then back to the front of the school. "Okay," he mumbled and emotion knitted her throat closed.

"Okay," she repeated and moved slowly toward the playground. Several women looked over as they approached, and she recognized a couple who'd been in her grade. They waved and she forced herself to breathe. If she panicked, Davey was likely to pick up on her energy. Already she could feel him dragging his feet behind her.

"We've got this," she said, glancing back at him.

He crossed his arms over his chest and stared at the ground.

Emily's heart sank but she kept the smile on her

face. All she wanted was to protect her sweet boy, but so often she didn't know how to help him.

Suddenly she heard a female voice calling her name. She looked up to see a tiny woman with a wavy blond bob coming toward her.

"I hoped you'd be here," Millie Travers said as she wrapped Emily in a tight hug. Millie was a recent addition to the community, having moved to town last year to be close to her sister Olivia. Both sisters were married to Crimson natives. Millie's husband, Jake Travers, was a doctor at the local hospital and Emily knew he had a daughter from a previous relationship who was around Davey's age.

Emily had met Millie, along with Katie's other girlfriends, at a breakfast Katie had coordinated shortly after her engagement. Her future sister-in-law was doing her best to make sure Emily felt included in her circle of friends, which she appreciated even if it was difficult for her to trust the bonds of new friendships after her experience in Boston. But she couldn't deny Millie was an easy person to like. "Katie told me to look out for you," the other woman said with a smile. "Your son is starting kindergarten this year, right?"

Emily swallowed. "Yes." She turned to where Davey stood stiff as a statue behind her. "Davey, this is Mrs. Travers, a friend of mine."

Her son stared at the crack in the sidewalk. Around the dull roar in her head, Emily heard the sound of laughter and happy shouts from the other kids on the playground. She wondered if Davey would ever be able to take part in such carefree fun.

If Millie was bothered by Davey's demeanor, she didn't show it. Instead, she sank down to her knees but kept her gaze on the edge of the sidewalk. "It's nice to meet you. My stepdaughter, Brooke, is starting first grade this year. She can answer any questions you have about kindergarten. Mrs. MacDonald, the kindergarten teacher, is really great."

"Whatcha doin', Mama-llama?" A young girl threw her arms around Millie's neck and leaned over her shoulder. Emily saw Davey's eyes widen. The girl wore a yellow polka-dot T-shirt and a ruffled turquoise skirt with bright pink cowboy boots. Her blond curls were wild around her head.

"I'm talking to my new friend, Davey," Millie said, squeezing the small hands wrapped around her neck. "He's starting kindergarten this year."

Brooke stood up and jabbed a thumb at her own chest. "I'm an expert on kindergarten." She stepped around Millie and held out a hand. "Ms. MacDonald has a gecko in her room."

"I have a question," Davey said quietly.

Brooke waited, reminding Emily a bit of Noah's puppy. Finally she asked, "What's your question?"

"Is it a crested gecko or a leopard gecko?"

"It's a leopard gecko and his name is Speedy," Brooke told him. "Come on. I'll take you to see the classroom."

Millie straightened, placing a gentle hand on Brooke's curls. "We need to make sure it's okay with Davey's mommy."

Emily was about to make an excuse for why Davey should stay with her when he slipped his hand into Brooke's. The girl didn't seem bothered by his rigid shoulders or the fact he continued to stare at the ground.

"I'll go, Mommy," Davey said softly.

Emily opened her mouth, but only a choked sob came

out. Biting down hard on the inside of her cheek, she gave a jerky nod.

"We'll be right behind you," Millie said, moving to Emily's side and placing an arm around her waist. "Go slow, Brookie-cookie. Show Davey the room and we'll meet you there so both Davey and his mommy can meet Ms. MacDonald."

"Okeydokey," Brooke sang out and led Davey through the crowd.

"Do you need a minute?" Millie asked gently.

Emily shook her head but placed a palm to her chest, her heart beating at a furious pace. "He doesn't usually…" She broke off, not sure how to explain what an extraordinary moment that had been for her son.

"Brooke will take care of him." Millie smiled. "He's going to be fine here. I know you don't have any reason to believe me, but something in this town rises up to meet the people who need the most help."

"I've never been great at taking help," Emily said with a shaky laugh. "I'm more a 'spit in your eye' type person."

"That's not what I hear from Katie. She's a very good judge of people. We'll follow them." Millie led her along the edge of the crowd, smiling and waving to a number of people as they went. But she didn't stop so Emily was able to keep Brooke and Davey within her sight. Millie's smile widened as she looked over Emily's shoulder. "And she's not the only one."

Emily turned to see a tall, blond, built man she recognized as Dr. Jake Travers, Millie's husband, walking through the parking lot with Jase at his side. Jase was a couple inches taller than Jake and his crisp button-down shirt and tailored slacks highlighted his broad shoulders and lean waist. Her heart gave a little leap and she smiled before she could stop herself.

"My husband is the hottest guy in town," Millie said, nudging Emily in the ribs. "But soon-to-be Mayor Crenshaw holds his own in the looks department. Wouldn't you agree?"

Emily shifted her gaze to Millie's wide grin and made her expression neutral. "He's my boss," she murmured.

The other woman only laughed. "I was Brooke's nanny when I first came to Crimson. That didn't stop me from noticing my *boss*." She gently knocked into Emily again. "Don't bother to deny it. Your game face isn't that good."

"My game face is flawless," Emily countered but the corners of her mouth lifted. Maybe not flawless when it came to Jase. The two men were almost at the playground. She leaned down to Millie's ear and whispered, "I'll only admit Dr. Travers is the second-hottest guy in town."

Millie hooted with laughter, then grabbed her husband and pulled him in for a quick kiss. "Jake, do you know Noah's sister, Emily?"

Jake Travers held out his hand. "Nice to see you, Emily."

"Your daughter was really nice to my son tonight," Emily told him. "She's a special girl."

He laughed. "A one-child social committee, that's our Brooke."

"She's giving Davey a tour of the kindergarten classroom," Millie told him. "How's the campaign, Jase?"

"Pretty good." Jase inclined his head toward the mass of kids on the playground. "But it's never too early to recruit potential voters." He smiled but Emily could see it was forced. Millie and Jake didn't seem to notice.

"Speaking of recruitment," Millie said, glancing up at Jake, who'd looped an arm around her slender shoulders. "I told the classroom mom you'd help coordinate a field trip to the hospital to see the Flight For Life helicopter." She turned to Emily. "She's working the volunteer table now so I'd like to stop by for a second. We'll see you in the kindergarten room. Brooke's classroom is right next door."

Emily nodded and kept moving toward the building. She saw Davey follow Brooke Travers inside.

"Campaign stop?" she asked Jase. He'd taken up Millie's post at her side and more people waved to him as they approached the school.

"I thought you and Davey might like some moral support." He shrugged, ducked his head, looking suddenly embarrassed. "Clearly, you've got it under control. He's made a friend and you—"

"I'm glad you're here," she said, letting out an unsteady breath. "Davey left my side, which was the whole point of this, and I almost broke down in tears on the spot." She stopped and pressed her open palm to his chest. His heart beat a rapid pace under the crisp cotton of his shirt. "Thank you for coming," she whispered.

He covered her hand with his, and then interlaced their fingers. "Anytime you need me," he said, lifting her hand and placing a tender kiss on the inside of her wrist.

Emily felt color rise to her cheeks, and she glanced around to find a few people staring at them. "Jase, we're..."

"At the elementary school," he said with a husky laugh. "Right." He lowered her hand but didn't release it.

Butterflies swooped and dived around Emily's stomach, and she felt like a girl holding hands with her first boyfriend. It took her mind off the worry of fitting in with the other mothers. Between Millie's exuberant welcome and Jase's gentle support, Emily felt hopeful she could carve out a happy life in the hometown that had once seemed too small to hold all of her dreams.

But the biggest dreams couldn't hold a candle to walking into the bright classroom to see her son solemnly shaking hands with his new kindergarten teacher.

"I'm glad Davey will be joining our class this year," the teacher said to Emily as she and Jase approached. "It's great he has a friend like Brooke to introduce him to the school."

Davey darted a glance at Emily and she saw his lips press together in a small smile when he spotted Jase next to her. "They have a Lego-building club," he mumbled, his eyes trained on Jase's shoes.

Jase crouched low in front of Davey. "That's excellent, buddy. Are you excited about school?"

Davey took several moments to answer. Emily held her breath.

Her son looked from Jase to her and whispered, "I'm excited."

Emily felt a little noise escape her lips. It was the sound of pure happiness.

Chapter Ten

Jase pulled up to his house close to nine that night. He parked his SUV in the driveway, then opened its back door for Ruby to scramble out. After the ice cream social, he'd gone directly to his dad's house with dinner.

Declan had gotten his cable fixed so they watched the season finale of some show about dance competitions, the point of which Jase couldn't begin to fathom. But his dad seemed happy and more relaxed than he'd been in ages. Ruby had curled up between them on the sofa and the quiet evening was the closest thing Jase could remember to a normal visit.

As soon as her legs hit the ground, Ruby took off for the house. Jase quickly locked the car, then came around the front, calling the puppy back to him.

But Ruby ignored him, too busy wriggling at the feet of the woman sitting on the bottom step of his front porch.

Emily.

She'd changed from the outfit she wore to the ice cream social to a bulky sweatshirt and a pair of…were those pajama pants?

"Hey," he called out, moving toward her. "These after-dark visits are becoming a habit with us."

She didn't answer or smile, just stood and stared at him.

Worry edged into his brain, beating down the desire that had roared to life as soon as he'd laid eyes on her.

"What's going on?"

She walked forward, her gaze intent but unreadable. When she was a few paces away, she launched herself at him. Her arms wound around his neck and he caught her, stumbling back a step before righting them both. She kissed him, her mouth demanding and so damn sweet. All of the built-up longing he'd tried to suppress came crashing through, smothering his self-control.

He lifted her off the ground, holding her body against his as he moved them toward the house. Ruby circled around them, nipping at his ankles as if she resented being left out of the fun. Emily's legs clamped around his hips as he fumbled with the house key. She continued to trail hot, openmouthed kisses along his jaw and neck.

"Are you sure?" he managed to ask as he let them in, then slammed shut the front door. "Is this—"

"No talking," she whispered. "Bedroom." She bit down on his lip, then eased the sting by sucking it gently into her mouth. Jase's knees threatened to give way.

He moved through the house with her still wrapped around him, and then grabbed a handful of dog treats from the bag on the dining room table as he passed.

He tossed them into the kitchen and Ruby darted away with a happy yip.

He felt Emily smile against his mouth. "Always taking care of business."

"You're my only business," he told her, moving his hands under the soft cotton of her sweatshirt as he made his way down the hall. He claimed her mouth again. "I want to taste every part of you." He pushed back the covers and lowered her to the bed, loving the feel of her underneath him.

"Later," she told him. "I need you, Jase. Now."

He lifted his head to meet her crystal-blue gaze but found her eyes clouded with passion and need. The same need was clawing at his insides, making him want to rip off her clothes like a madman. To think she was as overcome as he was changed something inside him. His intention of savoring this moment disappeared in an instant.

Straightening, he toed off his shoes, then pulled his fleece and T-shirt over his head in one swift move. Emily sat up, tugging at the hem of her sweatshirt and he was on the bed in an instant.

"Let me." As she lifted her arms, he pulled off the sweatshirt, leaving her in nothing but a pale pink lace bra. Lust wound around his chest, choking off his breath as he gazed at her. He felt like a fumbling teenager again, unable to form a coherent thought as he stared.

Her eyes on his, Emily reached behind her back and unclasped the bra, then let it fall off her shoulders and into her lap.

"Beautiful," Jase murmured as her breasts were exposed. He reached out to touch her and she scooted forward, running her hands over his chest.

"Right back at you," she said.

"Emily—"

"I want this," she told him. "I want you. Please don't make me wait any longer."

He wanted to laugh at her impatience. He'd been waiting for this moment for as long as he could remember. He stood again, shucked off his jeans while she shimmied out of her pajama bottoms and panties.

"Condom?" she asked on a husky breath when he bent over her again.

He started to argue, to insist they take their time but the truth was he didn't know how long he'd last if she continued to touch him. He opened the nightstand drawer and grabbed a condom.

She reached for it but he shook his head. "I better handle this part or the night will really be over before it starts."

Emily smiled and bit down on her lip, as if pleased to know she affected him so strongly. Was there really any question?

A moment later he kissed her again, fitting himself between her legs, capturing her gasp in his mouth as he entered her.

Nothing he'd imagined prepared him for the reality of being with Emily. She drew him closer, trailing her nails lightly down his back as they found a rhythm that was unique to them.

Everything except the moment and the feel of their bodies moving together fell away. All of life's complications and stress disappeared as passion built in the quiet of the room. In between kissing her, he whispered against her ear. Not the truth of his heart. Even in the heat of passion he understood it was too soon for that.

Instead he murmured small truths about her beauty, her strength and the complete perfection of being with her. She moaned against him, as if his words were driving the desire as much as the physical act. Her grasp on him tightened and he felt her tremble at the same time she cried out. She dug her nails into his shoulders and the idea that she might mark him as hers made his control shatter.

He followed her over the edge with a groan and a shudder, and she held him to her, gentling her touch as their movements slowed.

Balancing himself on his elbows, he brushed away loose strands of hair from her face. She looked up at him, the blue of her eyes so deep and her gaze painfully vulnerable. She blinked several times, her mouth thinning but her eyes remained unguarded. It was like the normal screens she used to defend herself wouldn't engage. He understood the feeling, so when she closed her eyes and turned her head to one side, he simply placed a gentle kiss on the soft underside of her jaw.

"No regrets," he murmured, then rose and walked to the bathroom. He glanced back to her from the doorway. Emily Whitaker was in his bed, the sheet tucked around her, her long blond hair fanned across his pillow like a golden sea. Tonight reality was indeed much better than his dreams.

Run, run, run.

The voice in Emily's head wouldn't shut up, and she pressed her fists against her forehead trying to press away the doubts blasting into her mind. She felt the wetness on her cheeks and couldn't stop the sobs that coursed through her body.

She wasn't sure how long she lay there before Jase returned. His fingers were cool around her wrists as he tugged them away from her face.

"No, Em." His voice was hollow. "No tears."

"I don't want to hurt you," she whispered, knowing she already had.

"If you mean hurt me with the best sex of my life, bring on more pain."

His kindness at this moment when he should hate her only made her cry harder. All the pain and sorrow and guilt and anger she'd bottled up during her marriage and before came pouring out. It was like being with Jase had torn away all of her emotional barricades.

"So not your best experience I take it," he said with a strained laugh.

She shook her head. "The best ever."

"Look at me and say that."

After several moments, she did. "It was amazing. You were amazing, Jase. I don't regret tonight, but I'm sorry."

"Remember I'm a simple man," he told her. "You're going to need to be a little clearer."

"I'm a mess." She used the edge of the sheet to wipe the tears from her face.

He nodded. "But a beautiful mess."

She poked at him. "You're not supposed to agree with me," she said but laughed at the fact that he had.

"Then I'm sorry. And we're even."

"We're not even." She didn't know how they ever could be. "You've been nice to me when I didn't deserve it, given me a job and connected to my son in ways not even his father could. I'm so grateful to you."

Jase raised an eyebrow. "So that was thank-you sex?"

She gasped and shifted away from him.

"I'm not complaining," Jase added, pulling her back again. "Just trying to figure out where we are here."

"You make me feel things," she whispered, scooting up so her back was against the headboard. She tucked the sheet more tightly under her arms, wishing she'd put on clothes while Jase was in the bathroom. He was wearing a pair of athletic shorts low on his hips but she still had the surprisingly awesome view of his ripped chest and broad shoulders. "Things I thought I put away to concentrate on the serious business of raising a son with special needs."

"Things like?"

She swallowed, worried her fingers together, traced the empty space on her left hand where she'd worn her wedding ring. She'd been so sure of herself when she'd met Henry. Positive that force of will could make her life perfect. Keep her heart safe. Impenetrable.

"Things like…joy…hope." There were other feelings that terrified her, but she wasn't ready to admit to anything more. She drew in a breath. "I came here tonight because I needed…"

"A release?"

"You."

The silence stretched between them, heavy with all they'd both left unspoken. He turned so he was sitting next to her and stretched his long legs out over the bed. "That's the nicest word I've ever heard."

He gathered her into his arms, sheet and all, his strong arms reminding her there was another kind of safety. The type that came from allowing another person to see her true self.

"I wanted you," she told him, circling one finger

through the sprinkling of dark hair across his chest. "I've wanted you since that day at the football game. Maybe since the morning of my mom's surgery when you came to the hospital."

She could feel his smile against the top of her head. "I've wanted you for as long as I can remember."

"But I'm empty, Jase. On the inside. There are a million broken pieces scattered there. I don't know how to fix them." She slid her hand up to his jaw, running her thumb over the rough stubble. "You deserve someone who is whole. I can't be that person yet, and I may never be the woman who can support you in all you do for this town. All people expect of you."

"You already have." He ran a finger along her back at the edge of the sheet. The simple touch was both soothing and strangely erotic. "You've organized my life, focused my campaign when I needed it and smoothed over the rough edges of having my dad involved. I've learned to rely on only myself, which is a difficult habit to end. But I trust you."

She shook her head. "I'll help with your message, not be part of it. I'm comfortable with a behind-the-scenes role. A friend. It's different."

"It doesn't have to be."

"I came here because you mean something to me, but I can't be the person you need." She reached up, pressed her mouth to his and repeated, "I *don't* want to hurt you." She meant the words but she couldn't admit the bigger truth—that she was terrified of her heart being the one to break. The more she cared, the harder the loss was to bear.

"There's more," Jase said softly. "Tell me why you're afraid."

"*I* don't want to be hurt," she admitted on a harsh breath. "I can't give you my heart because having it break again would kill me, Jase."

"I won't—"

"You can't know that." She tucked her head into the crook of his arm, unable to meet his gaze and say the words she needed him to hear. "My dad certainly didn't plan to die from cancer and leave my mom alone. I never thought I'd marry a man who couldn't accept his own son."

"I'm not your ex-husband." Jase's voice was pitched low.

"Henry isn't a villain. He's someone who needs his life to look perfect." She gave a strangled laugh. "I have no room to judge when it's what attracted me to him in the first place. Having a baby opened my heart in ways I didn't expect. I never wanted to feel that way, to be vulnerable. Davey is everything to me. But there isn't room for anyone else. I want you, and I don't regret coming here. But we can't let it go any further." She tried to pull away, but his arms tightened around her.

"What if this is enough?"

She stilled, risked a glance up to find him smiling at her. "Is that possible?" A piece of hair fell across his forehead, and she pushed it back, loving the feel of his skin under her fingers.

"I know it's not possible that once with you is enough for me." He lowered his mouth to hers, his lips tender. Desire pooled low in Emily's belly and she moved in his arms. The evidence she wasn't the only one affected pressed against her hip. She shifted again.

"Emily," he groaned against her mouth. "You're killing me."

"In a good way, I hope. I like being in your arms, Jase. I want to feel something. I'm tired of the nothingness. I want more. With you."

He moved suddenly and she was on her back again with Jase's body pressed to hers. "Then no worries, regrets or expectations."

"Expectations?"

"Expectations most of all." He pulled the sheet down, then skimmed his teeth over the swell of her breast. "I'm drowning under them, Em. But not with you. With you I can just *be*. And I promise you the same. We can be friends and more. But only as much as feels right. No other promises. No blame. No stress."

Another layer of joy burst to the surface inside her. It felt as if her chest was filled with bubbles, fizzy and light. She felt drunk with the exhilaration of it.

Right now, every part of her life was filled with stress. It was part of being a single mother. Even with her family's support, she could never truly let go. What Jase was offering felt like a lifeline. And the best part was she could give the same thing back to him. Pleasure for the sake of pleasure. No expectations.

It felt like freedom.

She wrapped her arms around his neck. "You've got yourself a deal, counselor."

"Sealed with a kiss," he said and nipped at the edge of her mouth.

"Sealed with a thousand kisses," she whispered and set about adding them up.

Chapter Eleven

The following Friday morning, Emily was busy untangling a strand of tiny twinkle lights being used to decorate the wide patio at Crimson Ranch, where tomorrow's wedding would be held. Sara worked on a separate length of lights while April Sanders arranged mason jars that would be filled with wildflowers on the tables set up around the patio.

Jase had closed the office today so they could both concentrate on wedding plans. Her mother was picking up Davey after school while April led a private yoga class for Katie and her girlfriends. The group would then go for facials and massages at a spa near Aspen before joining the men for the scavenger hunt Emily and Jase had organized. Emily had worked to make sure the activities leading up to the wedding were fun, personal and helped celebrate who Katie and Noah were as a couple.

She understood why they'd selected the ranch as their wedding venue. Located on the outskirts of town, the property had been beautifully restored in the past few years to become one of the area's most popular destinations.

In addition to the rough-hewn-log main house, there was a large red barn and several smaller cabins spread around the property. Clumps of pine and aspen trees dotted the landscape, giving the buildings a sense of privacy. Each time the breeze blew Emily enjoyed the sound of aspen leaves fluttering in the wind. She could see where the property dipped as it got closer to the forest's edge and knew the creek ran along the divide.

"You had sex." Sara grinned at Emily.

Emily spit the bite of muffin she'd picked up from the basket sitting on the table. "Excuse me?" She choked on muffin crumbs.

April patted her on the back. "Don't take offense. The more outlandish Sara's comments, the more she likes you."

Sara laughed and continued to string lights. "For the record, I like you a lot, Emily Whitaker. Not as much as I like your brother. When I first came to town, Noah flirted with me every chance he got."

"Noah flirted with everything with a pulse before Katie," Emily muttered.

"But with me he was trying to make Josh jealous." Sara's smile was devious. "You have points in your favor for being related to Noah, but there are other reasons I like you."

"You barely know me." Emily wiped the back of her hand across her mouth. "You definitely don't know me well enough to comment on my sex life." She heard the pretentiousness in her voice that she'd perfected during her short marriage.

Sara only laughed again. It was a rich, musical sound that projected across the vast pasture spreading out behind the house. Sara was petite with pale blond hair and luminous blue eyes. Her bigger-than-life presence made her hard to ignore. Emily supposed the "it girl" vibe contributed to Sara's fame from the time she'd been a child actor.

"We met at the dinner to celebrate your mom's recovery," Sara told her. "You were there with your son, and it's clear you're devoted to him. Another plus in your favor."

"I remember but—"

"You looked tense and defensive, like you might snap in two at any moment." Sara waved a hand toward Emily. "Now you're relaxed and you can't control the good-sex grin on your face—"

"I can control my smile," Emily argued, then thought of Jase and felt the corners of her mouth tug upward. She pressed her fingers to her mouth and glanced at April.

"Don't look at me. I'm certainly not smiling like that."

"Which is what we're working on next," Sara said, moving to April's side. "You've been alone for too long, my friend."

April shook her head, a tangle of red curls bouncing around her face. "One marriage was quite enough, thank you. I'm perfectly content without a man in my life."

"Don't forget I was married, too." Emily wasn't sure

why she felt compelled to argue this point. The idea that these women she was only beginning to know could read her was scary as hell. "I have a son and he's my priority. I don't have time for anything else."

"But you've been making time," Sara said.

April's voice was gentle. "You do seem happier, which is a good thing."

"Maybe it's the yoga." Emily pointed at April. "I've been coming to your classes. Maybe you should take credit for my newfound calm, if that's what I have."

"It's more than calm," April told her with a smile. "It's a glow. I'd love to believe it was the yoga but—"

"It's sex." Sara winked. "You don't have to admit it for it to be true."

"Don't tell Katie," Emily mumbled after a moment. "She and Noah will want there to be more to it than there is." She bit down on her lip, then grinned. "And it's great the way it is."

It had been more than great and her stomach did a slow, sweet roll at the thought of the time she'd spent with Jase. It was easy to have him come to the farm with Ruby after work under the guise of discussing wedding plans or the mayor's race, and he'd become a fixture at their dinner table. Emily's mother had even insisted he bring Declan to join them for several evening meals.

At first it amazed her how seriously he seemed to value her opinion. Whether on reception details or the more important campaign strategies, he listened to her ideas and often used them as the foundation from which to build his own.

Emily liked being someone's foundation. And she loved the private, stolen moments when Jase would wrap her in his arms and shower her with kisses. She felt the telltale goofy smile tug at her mouth again.

Sara threw an arm around April's shoulder. "Yoga classes are lovely but nothing is better than the restorative powers of great sex." She pointed at Emily. "Are you going to tell us who it is?"

"Do I have to?"

Sara thought about that for a moment. "No, but if you don't I'll be forced to ask your soon-to-be sister-in-law."

April lifted her hand to clamp it over Sara's mouth. "Forgive her. She means well. You don't have to tell us anything." April's voice was gentle, her tone so motherly it made Emily warm inside. "For the record," April added, "I think Jase is great."

"He is…" Emily narrowed her eyes. "Wait. That was sneaky." A gorgeous earth mother with a little edge.

"April's the worst," Sara said when April dropped her hand. "She's gentle and sweet, so people don't realize she's also whip smart and far too observant. The thing that makes it less annoying is she'll protect your secrets to her grave."

"Is Jase a secret?" April asked, her eyes all too perceptive.

"Yes." Emily shook her head. "I mean, no. We're friends."

"April needs a friend like that," Sara said with a laugh.

"Why don't you worry about your own love life and leave mine alone?" April crossed her arms over her chest and did her best to glare at Sara. She still looked sweet.

"No worries in my life." Sara wiggled her brows. "Josh is absolutely perfect. In fact, just last night…"

"Save it," April said quickly. "We're talking about Emily."

"Feel free to move on," Emily told them, then held up a hand to Sara. "I'm not asking for details about your private life."

Sara grabbed a muffin off the table and dropped into a chair. "You don't seem like a sell-it-to-the-tabloids type of person."

"No."

"Of course she's not," April agreed. "So you and Jase are friends." April pointed at Emily. "The kind of friends that have seen each other naked."

"That's one way to put it," Emily answered, making a face.

"You like him?"

Emily nodded.

"A lot?" Sara asked.

"Yes."

"Everyone in town loves him," April offered. "Why just friends and why the secret?"

"Because," Sara added, popping a bite of muffin in her mouth. "You understand this town can't keep a secret? People will find out."

"If they don't already know," April said.

"We want something that belongs to us."

Now Sara's face softened. "Oh, yes. I understand." She glanced at April. "We both do."

Sara stood and came to give Emily a hug. She glanced over her shoulder at April. "Come on. Group embrace."

The willowy redhead, who smelled of vanilla and cloves, wrapped them both in a tight hug. "What is between you and Jase is yours," she whispered. "But don't hold on to it too tight. Love is like a garden, Emily. It needs light and air to breathe, or it will shrivel before it has a chance to grow strong."

Emily gasped. "It's not love," she murmured. "It can't be."

Neither Sara nor April answered. They only tightened their hold on her.

By the time the last team came through the doors of the brewpub in downtown Crimson, Jase's mood was as dark as the mahogany paneling lining the walls.

Luckily his friends didn't seem to notice. Everyone had loved Emily's scavenger hunt. The teams had raced through Crimson collecting mementoes that were special to Noah and Katie.

Now they were sharing stories about the couple, laughing and toasting the impending nuptials as the bride and groom held court at one of the large tables in the center of the bar. The entire evening had been a success if he ignored the fact that Emily was doing her best to avoid him.

With so many of their friends around, it was easy to accomplish. No matter how many times Jase tried to meet her gaze or talk to her alone, she managed to slip away. He knew she'd spent the day working out at Crimson Ranch with Sara and April, but he couldn't imagine how things could have changed between them so quickly.

He watched her step away from the main group to take a call on her cell phone, her brows puckering at whatever was being said on the other line. The conversation only lasted a few minutes, and he moved behind her as she ended the call.

"Everything okay?"

She jumped, pressing a hand to her chest. "Sneak up much?"

"Avoid people much?" he countered.

Color rose to her cheeks and she looked everywhere but into his eyes. The sudden distance between them made him angry. This had been the best week of his whole damn life. Even with the campaign, work and all the other pressures of regular life, Jase had felt happier than he could remember. He wanted more from Emily. He wanted the right to give more *to* her.

Maybe it was excitement around the wedding or so many of his friends in relationships, but he was convinced Emily was meant for him. He'd always made decisions in his life based on what was smart and responsible. Duty had governed his actions for as long as he could remember. Being with Emily was about making himself happy. Making her happy. For the first time, he wanted to commit to something more than this town and restoring his family name.

He wanted something of his own.

He wanted Emily.

"It's been a hectic day," she said, her tone stiff. "I want everything to be perfect for Noah and Katie."

"I thought we agreed perfection is overrated."

She looked at him now, her eyes sad. "Not for the two of them. They deserve it."

"You deserve—"

She held up a hand. "I can't have this conversation now. My mom called. One of Davey's completed sets fell off the shelf and broke. He's having a meltdown." The sound of laughter and music carried to them and she glanced over his shoulder at their friends. She looked so alone it made his gut twist. "I've got to go, but I don't want to worry Noah. Will you cover for me?"

"Let me come with you."

"It's better if you don't," she whispered. "People will talk."

"I don't give a damn what anyone says."

She wrapped her arms tight around her middle. "I do."

Those two words killed him. He'd told her he wouldn't push her, and he had to honor that. When she turned to walk away, it took everything in him not to stop her.

Even more when Aaron Thompson slid off his bar stool as she moved past. The man put a meaty hand on Emily's arm and she flinched. Jase saw red as Aaron leaned closer and Emily's face drew into a stiff mask.

Jase was striding forward by the time she shook free and ran out the pub's front door.

"What the hell did you say to her?" He pushed Aaron's broad chest, and the man stumbled into the empty bar stool, knocking it on its side with a clatter.

Jase felt the gazes of the crowded bar on him, but for once he didn't care. He stepped into Aaron's space as the other man straightened.

Aaron leaned closer and lowered his voice so only Jase could hear. "I told her she'd have a hard enough time raising that weirdo kid of hers in this town without hitching herself to the Crenshaw wagon." His beady eyes narrowed farther. "When she's ready for a real man, she should give me a call. Your dad couldn't keep a woman satisfied, and I doubt you're any different."

It didn't matter that Emily was gone. Jase knew Aaron's words would have prodded at her fears, the same way they slithered into his. "Don't ever," he said on a growl, "speak to her again."

"Oh, yeah?" Aaron smirked. "Whatcha going to do about it?"

Jase hauled back his fist and punched Aaron, his knuckles landing against skin with an audible thud. The burly man staggered a few steps before righting himself. Noah and Liam had already grabbed hold of Jase.

"Dude," Aaron shouted into the sudden quiet of the bar. "I'm sorry. My dad wants what's best for this town. You don't have to threaten our family."

"Settle down, man," Noah said when Jase strained against him.

"He's lying." Jase felt blood pounding against his temples. He glanced around the bar to find himself the center of attention from every corner. He was so used to being universally liked, it took him a minute to recognize the emotions playing in the gazes of the friends and strangers who stared at him.

Anger. Disappointment. Pity.

"He's a liar," Jase yelled and felt a heavy hand clasp on to his shoulder.

"What's the problem?" Cole Bennett, Crimson's sheriff, stepped between Jase and Aaron.

Aaron winced. "I made an offhand comment about the election to Jase," he said, holding a hand to one eye. "You know, *may the best man win* and whatever. He went crazy on me." He looked at the sheriff all righteous indignation. "Must have hit a nerve. My dad can tell you plenty of stories about the Crenshaws going ballistic for no reason."

Anger radiated through every cell in Jase's body. He

shifted, then realized Noah and Liam were still holding him. "I'm fine," he said, shrugging away.

"You sure?" Noah's voice was concerned.

"Yeah." He pointed at Aaron. "That's not what went down and you know it."

Sheriff Bennett stepped closer to him, placing one hand on his chest. "You want to tell me a different side of the story?"

Jase opened his mouth, then snapped it shut again. He caught Aaron's smug gaze over Cole's shoulder and realized tonight was no accident. He'd been set up in this scene and had fallen right into the trap. He couldn't contradict Aaron's story without revealing specifics of the truth, which would humiliate Emily.

"No." He closed his eyes and tamped down his temper. "I've got nothing to say."

Cole heaved out a sigh. "Are you sure?"

Jase met the other man's gaze. "I am."

"What if I want to press charges?" Aaron asked.

Cole gave Jase an apologetic look, then turned to the other man. "Do you?"

"I should. It was a cheap shot." The bartender handed Aaron a bag of ice and he groaned a little as he pressed it to his eye. "But I guess we can't expect anything else from a Crenshaw."

Noah took a step forward, anger blazing in his eyes. "Don't be a—"

"It's okay," Jase interrupted, grabbing hold of his friend. "If he wants to press charges—"

"I don't. My father taught me to be the better man."

"Okay, then. Let's move on. Everybody back to their regularly scheduled evening." Cole turned to Jase. "I assume you're heading out?"

Jase nodded.

"I don't know what he did to deserve that punch," Cole said, "but I can guarantee it wasn't the story he told about the election. You sure you don't want to tell me anything else?"

"Positive."

With a nod, Cole moved away. Liam and Noah took his place.

"What the hell, Jase?" Noah asked. "I don't think I've ever seen you take a swing at somebody."

"I've got to get out of here," Jase muttered. "Sorry about causing a scene during your party."

Liam placed a hand on his shoulder. "You want company?" When Jase shook his head, Liam nodded and walked back toward their group of friends.

"Come back to our table," Noah told him. "Don't let this ruin the night."

"I'm not going to," Jase answered, "but I need to go now. Give Katie a hug for me. I'll pick you up in the morning to head out to Crimson Ranch."

Noah looked like he wanted to argue but only said, "No one expects you to be perfect, Jase."

"I know." But both of them knew it was a lie. People in this town expected perfection, duty and self-sacrifice from Jase, all of it offered with a smile. He understood that in the way of small towns, the news of the punch would spread like dandelion fuzz on the wind. The news, while inconsequential in its retelling, only needed to be nurtured a bit before it took root and grew into the start of a weed that could derail everything he'd worked to create.

At this moment he couldn't bring himself to care.

He left the bar and kept his head down as he walked to his parking space in the alley behind his office building. Driving out of town, he was tempted to take the turnoff toward the Crawfords' farm. Thoughts of Emily and her reaction to Aaron's taunts consumed him, but he'd promised not to ask her for more than she was willing to give. In his current mood he might drive a wedge between them if he pushed her.

Instead he steered his SUV toward the trailer park and pulled into his father's small lot. The blue-tinted glow from the television was the only thing lighting the inside of the trailer.

Declan hit the mute button on the remote when Jase walked in. "I thought the big party for Noah was tonight?"

"It is," Jase said, lowering himself to the sofa. "What happened to our family, Dad? Why are we so messed up? Mom leaving with Sierra, you and Uncle Steve drinking, Grandpa in jail. Why does every generation of our family have a sad story to tell?"

His father leaned back against the recliner's worn cushion. "Not every generation. Not you."

"Not yet," Jase shot back. "It's like there's a curse on us, and I don't know if I'm strong enough to break it."

"You already have."

"I decked Aaron Thompson tonight."

"Hot damn," Declan muttered. "That little jerk has been giving you grief since grade school."

"You noticed?"

"I'm a drunk, not an idiot. Hitting Aaron does not make you cursed. Hell, I've taken a swing or two at Charles over the years."

"And gotten yourself cuffed for the trouble."

"Worth it every time."

"I'm not you."

Declan laughed. "Praise the Lord." He leaned forward, placed his elbows on his knees. "In a town like Crimson, people see what they want. Once a reputation is set, it's hard to change it. I don't know how the trouble with our family started, but I do know it's easier to live down to expectations than to try to change them. At least it was for me. Your grandpa went to jail for the first time when I was ten. My brother and I had our first beers when we were eleven. Working in the mine didn't help. Nothing much good comes from sticking a bunch of ornery men inside a mountain."

Jase asked the question he'd been afraid to discuss with his dad for almost twenty years. "What about Mom?"

"Your mom was right to go. I was a mess back then."

"Yeah, Dad," Jase answered, "I know. I was the one taking care of you."

"You don't remember, do you?"

"Mom leaving?" Jase shrugged. He remembered crying. He remembered being alone at night staring at the empty bed where his sister had slept next to him.

"She wanted you to go with her."

"No. She took Sierra and left me behind."

"Because you told her I needed you more." When Declan met Jase's gaze, his eyes were shining with unshed tears. "She had your little suitcase in the trunk but you refused to get in the car. It killed her but eventually she agreed to let you stay. That's how I know you're not like the rest of us. You've never done a selfish thing in your life. You take care of this town like you've taken care of me all these years. With every ounce of who you are. You're not part of the curse. You're our family's shot at breaking it."

Jase closed his eyes and tried to remember the details of the night his mom had driven away. All he could see was Sierra's face in the car window and the taillights glowing in the darkness. The days after were a blur of tears and anger and his father going on a major bender.

"One punch doesn't make you a troublemaker, Jase."

"Tell that to the people who witnessed it."

"What I should do is talk to the man who's the cause of all your recent stress. This is Charles Thompson's fault. If he—"

"It's fine." Jase stood, ran a hand over his face. "Don't go after Thompson again. You're right. The Crenshaw curse ends with me."

He started to walk past his dad, but Declan reached out with a hand on Jase's arm. "It's what you want, Jase. Right?"

"Sure, Dad." Jase didn't know how else to answer and he was too tired to sort out his muddled emotions, either to his father or himself. "I'm picking up Noah early tomorrow to drive out to the ranch. Call if you need anything, okay?"

"Save me a piece of cake," his dad said, sitting back in the recliner. Declan had been invited to the wedding but since alcohol was being served, he'd decided to forgo the celebration. Jase appreciated his dad's effort to stay sober but hated that it isolated Declan even more than he already was.

"Are you sure you don't want me to get you for the ceremony?"

"Enjoy yourself tomorrow, son. Don't worry about me."

Jase gave the smile he knew his dad wanted to see. "Call if you change your mind."

Chapter Twelve

"Are you nervous?" Emily paced the guest cabin where she and Katie were waiting for the wedding to start. "You don't look nervous." She turned to Katie, who was glowing in the ivory gown they'd chosen at the bridal salon in Aspen. "You look beautiful." The satin gown had a sweetheart neckline and a lace overlay that was both delicate and modern. Katie's dark hair was pulled away from her face in a half-knot, with gentle curls tumbling over her shoulders. "Noah is going to lose his mind when he sees you. But, seriously, shouldn't you be nervous?"

Katie smiled and patted the bed next to her. "I don't need to because you've taken care of everything. It's perfect, Em. My dream day." As Emily sat down on the patchwork quilt, Katie took her hand. "Thank you for everything."

"It was easy." She gave a strangled laugh. "My mother-in-law and I were at the reception hall until two in the morning the night before my wedding redoing seating arrangements. There were so many stupid details to focus on but none of them involved preparing Henry and me to make a life together." She squeezed Katie's fingers. "You and Noah are doing this right."

"Unrequited love, fear of commitment, friendship and a baby after a breakup," Katie said with a laugh. "We might have had the order a little off."

"The love is what counts," Emily answered. She stood when Katie sniffed and Emily grabbed the box of tissues from the dresser, handing Katie a wad of them. "No crying. Your makeup is perfect."

"Then don't say sweet things to me." Katie dabbed at the edge of her eyes with a tissue. "I asked you for my dream wedding, and you've given it to me."

"Not quite yet."

A knock sounded on the door. "Ladies, are you ready?" Sara called.

"Perfect timing," Emily said with a smile.

Katie stood, her eyes widening as she pressed a hand to her stomach. "Wow. Just got nervous. Major butterflies."

"You've got this." Emily opened the door and followed Katie out, smiling as Sara oohed and aahed over the dress. Katie's father was waiting at the edge of the barn, out of sight of the chairs set up in front of the copse of aspens where the ceremony would take place. It was a perfect fall day, cool and sunny with just the slightest breeze.

She knew Katie and her parents weren't close, but her father became visibly emotional at the sight of his daughter. It made Emily's heart ache missing her own dad and all the moments she'd never get to share with him.

But this wasn't a day for sorrow, and she was honored to be Katie's maid of honor. She adjusted Katie's train and then stepped away. When the processional music began, she turned the corner from the barn toward the wedding guests. All Katie's and Noah's closest family and friends were in attendance. Emily's gaze sought Davey first, her son looking so handsome in his suit, standing next to his grandma in the front row. His eyes flicked to hers and she saw the stiffness in his small shoulders ease the tiniest bit.

The knowledge that seeing her gave him some comfort made her heart squeeze. She looked up to her brother standing in front of the grapevine arbor and smiled before her eyes met those of the man standing next to him.

She had to work to control her expression as Jase looked at her, his gaze intense. Her knees went weak and she clutched the bouquet of wildflowers tighter. One foot in front of the other, she reminded herself. Breathing in the warm mountain air, she felt her heart skip as Jase's mouth curved up at one end. As much as she'd tried to avoid him the previous night, now she couldn't break eye contact, even as she took her place in front of the assembled guests.

The music changed and Katie came into view. Emily glanced at the beautiful bride but then watched her brother's face as Katie moved closer. There was so much love in Noah's eyes. It was as if the whole world went still for a moment and there was only her brother and his bride. Emily was suddenly grateful for the tissue she'd stuffed under the ribbon of her bouquet.

She continued to need the tissue as the short ceremony progressed. By the time Noah leaned down to kiss his bride, Emily swore she could hear the whole valley choking back tears. Then there were only smiles and cheers as Noah and Katie walked back down the aisle hand in hand.

Jase offered her his elbow and she tucked her hand in it, blushing as he leaned close to her ear and whispered, "You look beautiful." She sucked in another breath and smoothed one hand over the pale pink cocktail gown she wore. She felt beautiful and happy and lighter than she had in ages. As they started down the aisle together, Emily was proud to meet the approving gazes of the people she'd come to think of as her community.

But Jase paused before the first row. "You two belong with us," he said to her mother and Davey.

Emily's heart, already so full, expanded even more at her mother's watery, grateful smile. Jase tucked Meg's arm into his other elbow and nodded at Davey. "Why don't you lead us down, buddy?"

The boy looked at the ground and Emily wanted to curse her own stupidity. She knew her son didn't like people looking at him and was afraid Jase's sweet gesture would backfire.

Davey chewed on his lower lip for a few seconds and finally muttered, "I'll follow you."

Emily breathed a sigh of relief and saw her mother do the same. Jase nodded and the four of them made their way past the other guests.

Emily didn't have a chance to speak to Jase alone until the dancing started. Meg and her new beau had taken Davey home after the cake was cut. To Emily's surprise, Davey had seemed to actually enjoy himself at the wedding, running around through the field behind the tables with the other kids.

He stuck close to Brooke Travers and didn't yell or play fight the way the other boys at the reception did, but he was definitely a part of the group and she couldn't have been prouder.

As the sky darkened over the mountain, silhouetting the craggy peaks against the deep blue of evening, a three-piece bluegrass band began to play. Noah pulled Katie onto the makeshift dance floor near the edge of the patio and other couples followed. Emily was just about to head inside to see if the caterers needed help packing up when strong arms slipped around her waist.

"Dance with me?" Jase asked but was already turning her to face him.

"I should check on things," she said but didn't protest when he lifted her hands to his shoulders.

"It's fine," he said, beginning to sway with her to the lilting sound of the fiddle drifting toward them. "Better than fine. All of your hard work made this a perfect day."

"We both worked hard," she corrected and rested her head against his chest. "You and I make a pretty good team." She was starting to trust the happiness she felt, to rely on it.

One of Noah's high school friends walked by, then stopped and clapped Jase on the shoulder. "Good to see you've grown a spine, Crenshaw."

Emily felt Jase tense and lifted her head.

He said a few words to the man, then tried to turn her away.

"Makes me want to vote for you all the more," the

man said with a chuckle. "I like a mayor with a strong right hook." With another laugh, he walked away.

Emily pulled back enough to look up at Jase. "What was that about?"

He shook his head. "Nothing."

"A strong right hook isn't nothing," she argued. "Did you hit someone?" She couldn't imagine a circumstance where Jase would throw a punch.

"Let's just dance."

"Tell me."

He blew out a breath. "Aaron Thompson," he muttered.

"What about him?"

"I saw him talking to you at the bar last night. You were upset when you left, so I asked him about it."

The happiness filling her moments earlier evaporated like a drop of water in the desert. Shame took its place, hot and heavy, a familiar weight on her chest. She hated that anyone, especially Jase, knew the awful things Aaron had said to her. But even more...

"You hit him?" she asked and several people nearby turned to look at them. She stepped out of Jase's arms and lowered her voice. "I didn't need you to defend me."

"He was out of line. No one has the right to speak to you that way." He reached for her, but she jerked back, giving herself a mental headshake. What was between her and Jase was supposed to be casual. Emily had let it turn into something more because he made her happy. But the way Aaron had taken advantage of that was the unwelcome reminder she needed. She couldn't let this go any further.

She caught Noah's gaze and flashed her brother a

small smile as she waved. "I'm going to check if the caterers need help."

"Emily," Jase whispered, "don't walk away."

But she hurried into the cabin before Jase could stop her. She told herself it was because she was angry at Jase, although it felt more like fear clawing at her stomach. Panic at the thought of depending on someone and allowing herself to be vulnerable again. Of needing Jase and then having him leave her. It was one thing when they were on equal ground, but if she began to rely on him and truly opened her heart…what was to stop him from breaking it?

April was supervising the last of the cleanup so Emily pitched in where she could. Her hands trembled as she moved vases of flowers to the kitchen's large island but she didn't stop working.

"I think we're almost finished in here," April said eventually. "I don't have a hot guy waiting to dance with me, so I can handle the rest."

"It's fine," Emily muttered. "I'm not in the mood to dance."

"Uh-oh." April stepped in front of her as she turned for the sink. "What's wrong?"

"Nothing."

"What kind of nothing?"

Emily sighed and met the redhead's gentle gaze. "Is it really possible to start over?"

April opened her mouth, then shut it again as if she didn't actually know how to answer the question.

"It seems easy in theory," Emily continued. "Cut out the bad parts from your life and move on. Let go. Tomorrow's a new day. I can spout out greeting-card sentiments until I run out of breath. But is it possible?

How can I leave the past behind? Life isn't simple, you know?"

"I do know," April said with a sad smile. "Maybe it's not about a fresh start as much as it is continuing to try to do better."

"Learn from your mistakes?" Emily laughed. "Another cliché, but I have plenty to choose from."

April picked up a flower and twirled the stem between her fingers. "Play it cool as much as you want, but it's obvious you really care for Jase, and he's crazy about you."

Emily swallowed. "I wasn't looking for…"

"For love?"

"It isn't—"

April tapped Emily on the nose with the wildflower's soft petals. "I have no history in this town, Emily. No expectations of who either of you are supposed to be. You can be honest with me."

"Which may be easier than being honest with myself."

"Start with saying the words out loud."

Emily swallowed then whispered, "I love him."

"I have a feeling he feels the same."

"He can't," Emily said, shaking her head. "We want different things from life. I can't be the woman he needs."

"Maybe what he needs is the woman you are."

Emily felt tears clog the back of her throat. A tiny sliver of hope pushed its way through the dark layers of doubt she'd heaped on top of it. "Are you always this good at giving pep talks?"

"To other people," April told her, "yes."

The catering manager walked back into the kitchen with the final bill.

"I'll take care of this," April said. "You find Jase."

"I can't tell him yet." Emily fisted her hands until her nails left marks on the center of each palm. "It's too soon. I don't know—"

"You might start with showing him how you feel," April said and nudged her toward the patio door.

"Right. Show don't tell. I think I can do that." At the thought of being in Jase's arms again, her stomach buzzed and fluttered like a thousand winged creatures were taking flight inside it. "I think I'd like that very much."

As she stepped back outside, she saw that Jase and the other guests had gathered in the center of the patio to say goodbye to Noah and Katie. The newlyweds were staying in one of the guest cabins at Crimson Ranch overnight before driving to the Denver airport tomorrow to fly out for their honeymoon to a Caribbean island.

"I'm so happy to have a sister," Katie said as Emily hugged her.

"Me, too," Emily whispered, then turned to her brother. "I'd tell you to get busy making me a little niece or nephew," she said, punching him lightly on the arm, "but for once in your life, you're an overachiever."

"Always the clever one." Noah chuckled and pulled her in for a hug. "Call if you need anything."

"I absolutely won't," Emily shot back. "You've earned these two weeks in paradise. Enjoy them."

"I intend to and thanks again, Em." Noah tipped up her chin. "You made my bride very happy."

"Go." Emily made a shooing motion. "I've laid all the groundwork for you to get lucky tonight."

Noah leaned in close and kissed Emily on the cheek. "Maybe I'm not the only one," he whispered with a wink, then turned and scooped Katie off her feet.

Everyone cheered as the couple disappeared down the pathway toward the far cabins. As the music started again, guests drifted back toward the patio. Emily continued to stare into the darkness for several minutes, nerves making her skin tingle as she thought about finding Jase in the crowd.

With a fortifying breath she turned and bumped right into him. She yelped and stumbled back. Jase grabbed hold of her arms to steady her.

"Were you some kind of a cat burglar in another life?" she asked, trying to wrestle her pounding heart under control. "You're far too good at being quiet."

He let go of her, dropping his hands to his sides. "My dad wasn't much fun with a hangover. I learned to be quiet so I wouldn't wake him."

"Oh." Her comment had been meant as a joke. The way he answered made her remember they'd each been shaped by their past. "I'm sorry."

"No need," he said quickly. "It's a fact."

"I meant for earlier. Even if it wasn't necessary, thank you for defending my honor with Aaron."

"Again, no need. You don't deserve to be dragged into the long shadow cast by my family's reputation." The music picked up tempo and Jase turned for the house. "Should we head back?"

Emily didn't move. "What do you mean your *family's reputation*? Aaron told me I might as well be campaigning for his father since I was distracting you from the usual attention you pay to Crimson and its residents. He insinuated that a relationship with a divorced mom of a kid with special needs would work against your bid for mayor."

"I'm going to kill him," Jase muttered. "I wish I would have knocked him out cold." He ran his hands through his hair, leaving it so tousled Emily couldn't resist reaching up to straighten it.

"No," she told him. "You shouldn't have hit him at all."

He pulled her hands away from his hair, clamping his fingers gently around her wrists. "Emily, what is the real problem here?"

Where to start?

Your dreams. My fears.

Falling in love with you.

Definitely don't lead with that one.

She raised up on tiptoe and slid her lips along his, the knot of tension inside her unfurling at the warmth of his mouth and the roughness of his stubble when their cheeks brushed. He smelled like the mountains and tasted of mint and sugary wedding cake. Right now, he was everything she wanted in the world.

Show don't tell.

"The only problem is we're not undressed."

Jase gave a harsh laugh. "You're trying to distract me."

"Is it working?"

"Hell, yes." He glanced over his shoulder toward the lights of the party, which was still going strong even in the absence of the bride and groom. "Think anyone will notice if we sneak away?"

"Let them notice." She would deal with the consequences of her feelings for Jase another time. When he laced his fingers with hers, Emily almost forgot her doubts. She simply let them go.

Giving in to the happiness fizzing through her made her giggle.

Jase glanced down at her but didn't stop moving toward his SUV. "What's so funny?"

She shook her head. "Nothing. I'm glad to be with you."

He opened the passenger door and she slipped in. "You just made me the second-happiest guy on this ranch." He pulled the seat belt around her, using it as an excuse to kiss her senseless.

She took out her phone and punched in a quick text to her mother as Jase came around the front of the SUV. "Everything okay?" he asked, turning the key in the ignition.

Emily waited to speak until her mother's answering text came through. Then she smiled at him. "I've got permission for a sleepover."

"The whole night?" His voice was husky.

"Yep. I mean, I'd like to be home in the morning for breakfast. Davey usually sleeps until about eight on the weekend so that gives us…"

"All night long," Jase finished, taking her hand and lifting it to his mouth. Then he cringed a little. "Unfortunately, the puppy doesn't like to sleep in so late."

"I guess you're going to have to make waking up early worth my while."

Of course, Ruby needed some attention when they got back to the house. "One of my neighbors came over a couple of times today to let her out and play with her." Emily laughed as Ruby exploded out of her crate, yipping and running circles around Jase as he struggled to clip on her leash. "Clearly, she's ready for more. I'm sorry. This isn't exactly a great start to a romantic evening. I need to take her for a short walk so she won't be so wound up."

"I'll come with you." They followed the puppy into the front yard toward the sidewalk.

As Ruby sniffed a tree, Jase shrugged out of his coat and wrapped it around Emily's shoulders. She loved being surrounded by his scent and the warmth of him. They started down the sidewalk with Ruby happily trotting next to them. She seemed in no hurry to do her business tonight, making Jase groan and Emily laugh.

"I'm sor—"

"Don't say it." She took his hand as they walked. "This is nice. I love the quiet of your neighborhood and this time of night, especially after the past week of planning the wedding. It feels normal."

"Normal is underrated," he said with a laugh. "Every birthday wish when I was a kid was for a normal family like yours."

"As I remember, a lot of those birthdays were spent at our house."

"Your mom would bake a red velvet cake and you'd refuse to come out of your room to sing."

Emily pressed her free hand to her face. "I was horrible to you."

"You were pretty mean to Noah, too, so I took it as a compliment."

"Only you, Jase."

Ruby finally found the perfect patch of grass and they turned back toward the house. They walked in silence for a few feet until Emily felt Jase's body tense.

"What is it?"

"I wanted to ask you something, a favor really," he told her. "You know city council is holding a town hall meeting in two weeks. Charles and I are both supposed to be there. People will have a chance to ask us questions about our plans as mayor."

She nodded.

"They'll want us to introduce our families as part of the meeting. I think it was Charles's idea as a way to discredit me. He can stand up there with his wife and sons as proof he's an established family man and I'll just be…alone."

"I'm sure your dad will come if you ask him."

Jase shook his head. "He doesn't like crowds. They make him anxious and that makes him want to drink." He let out a small laugh. "Well, everything makes him want to drink but so far he seems committed to his sobriety this time around. I don't want to mess that up."

"You've supported him in so many ways over the years," Emily argued. "He can do this for you."

"Honestly, I'm not sure if having my dad there would be a help." Jase stopped at the bottom of his porch steps as Ruby nosed around in the bushes in front of the house. "I was hoping you and your mom and Davey would stand up for me."

Emily felt her mouth drop open and quickly snapped it shut at the look of disappointment that flashed in Jase's eyes.

"Never mind. Stupid idea." He let go of her hand to scoop up the puppy. "When you mentioned me celebrating my birthdays at your parents' farm, it made me think the Crawfords were almost more of a family to me than my own." Ruby wriggled in his arms and licked his chin. "But you aren't my family, and I know how you feel about being in the spotlight. I'll bring Ruby." He laughed, but it sounded forced. "Puppies are always crowd pleasers."

He turned for the house, then stopped when she placed a hand on his arm.

Show don't tell.

Emily had assumed April meant those words from a physical standpoint, which was easy enough. She wanted Jase more than she could have imagined— longed to be in his arms. She thought about all the little things he'd done for her, from allowing her full control of his office to letting her take the lead on the wedding plans to showing up at the school ice cream social to check on her and Davey.

Despite her fears and doubts, she wanted to give something back to him. The town hall meeting was big, but she was coming to realize starting over was a mix of baby steps and giant leaps. Not pretending the past didn't happen but moving through the old hurts to create new happiness.

"We'll be there," she said and had the pleasure of watching gratitude and joy wash over his features. It felt so good to give this to him. It felt right.

"You don't have to," he told her. "I mean it. I'll be fine."

"You're not alone," she whispered. She leaned forward to kiss him but stopped when Ruby licked her right on the mouth.

Jase groaned as Emily laughed.

"You should still bring the dog," Emily said as she wiped her mouth. "She's your ace in the hole."

"Right now I want her out of my arms." He nudged

open the front door and deposited the puppy on the hardwood floor. "And you in them." He pulled Emily against his chest.

"I take priority over Ruby?" she asked with a laugh. "I feel so important."

"You take priority over everything," he whispered against the top of her head. His words made sparks dance across her skin. "Thank you, Em. I know what I'm asking is a lot." He tipped up her head, cupping her face between his hands. "If you decide it won't work, I'll understand."

His touch was tender. "I'll make it work," she told him and somehow she would.

Ruby scampered toward her basket of toys, picked up a stuffed bunny with her, teeth then walked into her crate to curl up with it.

"She's tired," Emily said.

"Finally."

Jase went over and locked the crate, then returned to Emily. "So how about a sleepover?"

Emily giggled. "Maybe you shouldn't call it that. It reminds me of being a kid...you know, pillow fights and nail-painting parties."

"Pillow fights, yes." Jase kissed the corner of her mouth. "Nail painting, no." He moved closer and deepened the kiss. She held on to him and he lifted her as if she weighed nothing, moving down the hall toward his bedroom. "Do you want to have a pillow fight?" he asked as he set her down on the bed, then covered her body with his.

"Maybe later."

"I'll hold you to that," he told her. "After I hold you to me."

She laughed again, loving how Jase made everything fun. She'd never thought of the bedroom as a place for laughter until the tall, sweet man watching her from chocolate-brown eyes had come into her life.

She slipped off her shoes and reached behind her back for the zipper of the cocktail gown she wore. Her fingers paused as Jase pulled his tie over his head, then undid the buttons of his tailored shirt. His broad chest made her mouth water.

He moved to the edge of the bed and slid his palms up her bare legs. He grasped the hem of her dress and she lifted up onto her elbows as he tugged it off her. His eyes darkened as they raced over her.

"The lingerie," he said in a half growl, "I like it."

Emily whispered a silent prayer of thanks to her new sister-in-law. Katie had insisted she buy the matching bra and panties during one of their prewedding shopping trips to Aspen. At the time it had seemed like a foolish expense, but now the lavender lace made her feel beautiful. Or maybe it was the way Jase was looking at her. Her whole body grew heavy with need.

She crooked a finger at him. "Come closer, Mr. Almost Mayor, and take it off me," she whispered.

He toed out of his shoes and took off his suit pants, then climbed onto the bed, lowering his weight over her as he claimed her mouth. No more joking or laughter. His kiss was intense and demanding, and she moaned as his fingers skimmed across her breast. Emily arched off the bed as his mouth followed, grazing the sensitive peak with his teeth.

Then they were a tangle of arms and legs, sighs and whispered demands. The demands came mostly from her. She was impatient for him but he insisted on moving slowly, savoring each moment and lavishing attention on every inch of her body.

This man wrote the book on show don't tell. She'd never felt so cherished or been so fully possessed. As much as she longed to say the words *I love you*, Emily still held back. But when they moved together as the pleasure built and built and finally shattered them both, all of her defenses crumbled in a shimmer of light and passion. She knew things could never go back to the way they'd been, at least not for her. Jase Crenshaw well and truly owned her heart.

Chapter Thirteen

Jase could feel Emily's heart beating steady against his chest early the next morning. She was wrapped around him, snuggled in tight and sleeping soundly.

She'd told him sleep was often elusive for her, so he reveled in the fact that she was snoring softly as morning light peeked in between the slats of the wood shutters that covered his bedroom windows.

He'd never allowed a woman to spend the night at his house before Emily. This place was a sanctuary to him, and he hadn't been willing to share it with anyone else. The satisfaction he felt at waking up with her beside him should be terrifying. It proved he was already in far too deep when he still expected her to break his heart.

Yet his smile wouldn't fade. It felt so damn *right* to have her here. He'd put the down payment on the modest bungalow shortly after taking over the law practice.

It had been a rite of passage to buy a home he could call his own. But he wasn't sure how to be a host and the women he dated invariably wanted to take over the role. Minutes in the door and they began rearranging sofa pillows and suggesting wall colors.

So he'd stopped inviting anyone over but his guy friends. They didn't care his walls were bare and he had nothing but leftover carryout and beer in the fridge. To his surprise, Emily hadn't either. He'd even solicited her opinion on what he should do to make it homier. She'd told him to keep it as it was, which had been both refreshing and disconcerting. Especially given the ruthlessness with which she'd taken over his office.

At first he'd thought she was respecting his space but over the past few weeks, when she'd stop by but never stay, he'd wondered if it was more about her keeping what was between them casual. Now she was here, and it seemed like a damn good first step.

"I can hear you thinking," she mumbled sleepily, rolling off him.

"Good morning," he said and kissed her cheek.

She yawned, her eyes still closed. "What's got the wheels turning so hard this early?"

"Paint colors."

"Is that code for kinky morning sex?"

He laughed and pulled her close again. "Would you like it to be?"

"Talk to me about paint colors."

He combed his fingers through her hair, loving its softness and the way the scent of her shampoo drifted up to him. "I need to update the house, make it more mine. I was thinking about what color to use for the family room and kitchen."

She rose onto her elbows. "While we're in bed together? What does that say about me?" She frowned but amusement flickered in her blue eyes.

"It says you inspire me to be a better person. Painting has been on the list for years, but I've ignored it. Even though I bought the house, I couldn't quite believe I deserved it. You make me believe."

Her gaze softened. "You make the most unromantic topics into love poems."

He tapped one finger against her nose. "Again, I give credit to you for inspiring me. Can we get back to kinky morning sex?"

"Dorian Gray."

He thought about that for a moment and then shook his head. "As in *The Picture of...*? The creepy book and movie?"

"Yes and no." She flipped onto her back again. "It's also a paint color, the perfect gray. You should use it for your family room and a shade lighter in the kitchen. It faces north so needs more light."

Jase felt a smile curve his lips. "You've been thinking about colors for my house."

Clearly misunderstanding, she crossed her arms over her chest. "You asked," she said on a huff of breath.

He levered himself over her and kissed the edge of her jaw. "Paint talk as foreplay. Works for me. What do you know about the color wheel?"

"I know you're crazy," she said, rolling her eyes.

"Only for you, Em."

She suddenly turned serious. "This isn't casual anymore."

He thought about lying so he wouldn't chase her away, but he couldn't manage it. "It's not casual for me," he agreed. "It never has been. We can still take it slow and I—"

She pressed her fingers to his mouth. "I like it slow." Her hand curled around to the back of his neck and she drew him down for a hot, demanding kiss. "I like it most ways with you."

"Emily," he said on a groan. "Tell me you're good with where this is going." He lifted his head and stared into her eyes. "I need to know."

She closed her eyes for a moment and took a deep breath. Then she looked at him again. "I'm scared of feeling too much. But I..." She paused, bit down on her lip, then whispered, "I want it to be more than casual. I want to try with you, Jase. For you."

"For us," he said. There was more he wanted to tell her, but she wasn't the only one afraid of being hurt. Jase was used to keeping the things he wanted most locked up tight. It was when he said the words out loud that his life usually went to hell.

Mommy, don't leave. Don't take Sierra.

Dad, stop drinking before it ruins you.

His requests met with disappointment so he didn't make them, and he wasn't going to now. He needed time to believe this precious thing between them wasn't going to be taken away.

He smiled and kissed her again. "We've got approximately not many minutes until the puppy starts whining," he said, glancing at the clock on the nightstand. "We've established slow is good. Now let's see how we do with fast."

The next two weeks flew by for Jase. One of his biggest cases went to trial early at the courthouse in Aspen, so he was out of the office most of the time. He'd never been as grateful for Emily, who managed his practice with so much efficiency he didn't worry about anything falling behind while he was in court.

He was even more grateful for her when he got home at the end of each long day. She'd taken over Ruby's care, picking up his energetic puppy in the morning on her way to the office and keeping her all day. She claimed both Davey and Tater, Noah's dog that was staying at the farm during Noah and Katie's honeymoon, loved having the puppy around.

When he could manage it, Jase drove directly to the farm after work. It was like he was a teenager again, showing up for dinner at Meg's big table, only now Emily greeted him with a kiss each time he arrived.

Everything in his life was exactly where he wanted it. Everything but the mayor's race. Charles was taking full advantage of Jase's busy schedule by planning campaign events all over town. Almost overnight, yard signs with the slogan Charles Thompson, A Family Man You Can Trust had popped up on every corner. Jase got calls from friends and business owners, suggesting he ramp up his efforts with the election date quickly looming.

The problem was he didn't want to take time away from the rest of his life to focus on the campaign. He couldn't stop questioning the reasons he'd decided to run for the position in the first place. Yes, he was dedicated to Crimson, but he didn't need to be mayor to prove that. Or did he?

He was getting pressure to be seen around town when all he wanted was to spend his free time with Emily and Davey. Although the boy was adjusting to school, he still preferred the quiet of home. Jase had set up a Lego construction area in the corner of his family room so Davey was becoming more comfortable at his house. That didn't solve the issue of Emily needing a quiet life with her son, while Jase's obligations to the town pulled him to be more visible with every passing day.

He checked his watch for the fifth time as he waited for the city council meeting to end late on Tuesday, one day before the big town hall event. Monthly council meetings were held in the evenings because so many of the members also had day jobs. Jase had never minded before because his life was the town. But Emily had texted that Davey wanted to show him his latest Lego structure, and he'd hoped to get out early enough to make it to the farm.

The council members continued to debate the date for the lighting of the town Christmas tree in December while Jase's mind raced from thoughts of Emily to the trial to the doctor's appointment he needed to reschedule for his father to the campaign he was pretending didn't exist.

"Jase, do you have anything to add?" One of the longtime council members lifted a thick brow.

Jase blinked and glanced around at his fellow council members, reluctant to admit he had no idea where the thread of the conversation had gone. Liam Donovan met his gaze and gave a subtle shake of his head.

"No," Jase said firmly, as if he knew what the hell they were talking about now. "I agree on this one."

Thankfully, the general comment was enough to satisfy everyone and the meeting adjourned. He checked his phone, disappointment washing through him. He'd missed a text from Emily, telling him Davey was going to bed and they'd keep Ruby overnight at the farm. She'd added an emoji face blowing a kiss at the end, which only made him want to hurl the phone across the room.

Jase didn't want emoji. He wanted Emily in his arms.

He punched in a quick text promising to stop by in the morning before heading to Aspen.

"You realize you can't speed up or slow down time by watching the clock," Liam said from behind his shoulder.

Gathering his things, Jase turned and shook his head. "It's a damn shame, too. Thanks for saving my butt just now."

Liam nodded. "You weren't exactly dialed in for this meeting. I'll walk out with you."

Jase watched a group of council members standing on the far side of the conference table, heads together as they talked. Charles Thompson was in the middle, as if holding court, and the sight made a sick pit open in Jase's gut. One of the men glanced back at Jase, guilt flashing in his gaze before he waved.

"Looks like you weren't the only one to notice." He followed Liam out into the cool autumn night. He should be sitting on his back porch with Emily right now. Instead he was heading over to his office to work a few more hours on the cross-examination he was preparing for tomorrow.

"Also looks like your campaign is in the toilet," Liam said without preamble. "Before you got to the meeting, Charles made a pretty convincing speech about you being pulled in too many directions to give your full attention to the duties of mayor."

"Which is not true—"

"He also hinted that your dad is having problems and you've got too many distractions right now."

Jase cursed under his breath and turned on his heel. The town meetings were open to the public so Charles had every right to be there. But not to spread lies about Jase's father. "My dad is fine," he ground out, moving back toward the courthouse. "I'm going to—"

"Whoa, there." Liam placed a hand on Jase's shoulder. "It's not a coincidence Charles showed up tonight, made the comment and now is hanging out after the meeting. He's playing dirty, Jase."

"Why the hell did you tell me, then?"

"Because *you* have a choice to make."

Jase shrugged away from Liam's grasp and paced several steps before turning and slamming his palm against the side of the brick building. He cursed again and shook out his hand. "I've made my choice."

"I'm new to the council," Liam said, "but from what I've heard, the choice was made for you. When the former mayor took off, Marshall Daley stepped in as mayor pro tem. He was never going to seek another term, so the town council members suggested you run."

"That's the basic gist," Jase admitted. "It wasn't supposed to be this complicated."

"Did you ever really want to be mayor?"

"Of course I did. I can do the job."

"I'm not debating that."

"I love this town."

"Again, you'll get no argument from me there. Hell, you had a major impact on my decision to make Crimson the headquarters for LifeMap. But it felt different. You were on a mission to make a name for yourself. I didn't understand it then…"

"And now you do?" Jase sagged against the building, tired at the thought of rehashing his family history one more time. "Everyone around here thinks they know me."

Liam shrugged. "It's clear you don't want it the way you once did."

"Is it so wrong to also want a life for myself, as well?"

"No."

"I won't let Charles win."

"Even if it means you lose in the long run?"

Jase straightened. "I'm going to make sure that doesn't happen."

"How?"

"Can I make a suggestion?"

Both men turned as Cole Bennett stepped out around the street corner.

"Evening, Sheriff," Jase said. "Out for a stroll downtown or is this official business?"

Cole moved closer. He wore jeans and a T-shirt and held up his hands, palms out. "Off duty tonight. I was hoping to talk to you before the town hall meeting this week." He glanced at Liam. "It's private."

Jase started to argue but Liam held up a hand. "I need to get home anyway. Let me know if I can help. No matter what you decide."

"Thanks, man." Jase shook Liam's hand, then watched him walk across the street to where his truck was parked.

"You have some advice for me?" he asked the sheriff.

"Information," Cole clarified. "Your office is on this block, right?"

Jase nodded.

The sheriff glanced over his shoulder. "Let's go there."

"Why do I have a bad feeling about this?" Jase asked as he led Cole a few storefronts down until they reached his office.

"Because you're not stupid," Cole answered bluntly.

With a sigh, Jase unlocked the door and flipped on the light in the reception area. The scent of vanilla from the candle Emily burned at her desk filled the air, and his heart shifted. The subtle changes she'd made to his life mattered and he hated that his sense of duty to the town was keeping them apart.

It wasn't only his schedule. They'd agreed their relationship wasn't casual, but he could feel Emily holding back. He assumed it was because of his increasing commitments to work and the campaign. While he wanted to tell her it would pass, how could he make that promise if he won the election?

"Since you're not on the clock, how about a drink?" Jase asked, moving toward his office. "I've got scotch or…scotch."

Cole chuckled low. "I'll have a scotch. Thanks."

Jase motioned him into the office, then went to the kitchenette area and poured two squat glasses with the amber-colored liquid. Back in the office, he handed one to Cole, then sat behind his desk.

Cole took a slow sip before placing the glass on Jase's desk. "How bad do you want to win the election?"

The question of the hour. "Not bad enough to do something illegal for it." It was the most honest answer Jase could give without exposing the doubts plaguing him.

"What about exposing something your opponent had

done?" the sheriff asked. "Not exactly illegal but it's definitely borderline. Turns out Thompson had been going easy on his friends and neighbors for years. Anytime there was a problem with someone he knew personally, the issue disappeared."

Jase actually laughed. "Everyone except my father."

Cole shrugged. "There's a lot of politics involved in small-town law enforcement. I'm overhauling the department, but I do have records that certain procedures weren't exactly…aboveboard when he was in charge."

"What are you going to do with the information?"

"That's why I'm here. Charles Thompson was supposed to retire and go fishing or whatever the hell else he wanted. I didn't take his bid for mayor too seriously at first." He picked up his glass of scotch and tipped it toward Jake. "You had the blessing of the council, so there was no question you'd be elected."

Jase didn't shy away from Cole's scrutiny. "Now there is?"

The sheriff finished off his scotch before answering. "Thompson is pushing you hard and you're letting him. I don't know if it's because the garbage he's throwing is getting to you or because you've decided you don't care about winning."

"Maybe I'm tired of my whole life revolving around Crimson."

"Fair enough, but I'm asking you to get your head back in the game. We need you, Jase. We need somebody decent in charge of this town." Cole placed his glass back on the desk and stood. "I can leak what I know about Thompson, make him go away, but it won't change how he's trash-talking you or what it means if you don't answer the accusations. You have a chance to tomorrow night. I hope you take it, but if you need something more let me know."

"Thank you," Jase said and watched the sheriff walk out the door. He threw back the rest of his scotch, welcoming the burn in his gut. Maybe he had been ignoring the campaign in the hope the decision would be taken from him. But that wasn't who he was, and Cole's visit proved it.

Why couldn't he have Emily and the mayor's position? Yes, she had doubts but he'd worked too hard to give up now. He needed to prove that she and Davey fit into his life, every part of it. The town hall meeting would be the perfect place to do just that.

Emily stopped in front of the entrance to the Crimson Community Center where the town hall meeting was about to start. She smoothed a hand over the fitted dress she hadn't worn since she'd stood next to her ex-husband when he'd made partner at his law firm.

"I should have picked something else. This is way too formal."

Her mother squeezed her hand. "You look lovely and the sweater softens the look." Meg glanced down at Davey, who stood a few steps behind Emily, his hands tightly fisted at his sides. "You are very heroic tonight."

Emily shared a look with her mom, then smiled at Davey. He'd insisted on changing into his superhero costume after school today and refused to put on a different outfit for the meeting. She understood that sitting still in a crowd of strangers was going to be a challenge, so hoped Jase understood Davey's wardrobe choice. Her purse was stocked with Davey's favorite snacks, a small bag of Lego pieces and the fail-safe iPad loaded with a few new apps. She prayed it would be enough to keep him content during the meeting.

As her mother held open the door, Emily put a hand on Davey's shoulder to guide him, then drew back as he flinched away from her touch.

Breathe, she told herself. Smile.

She'd come back to Crimson for a quiet life, and now she was putting herself on display for the entire town. Her mother led them up the side aisle to the front row of chairs marked Reserved. Emily glanced over her shoulder as she took her seat and saw several of her new friends sitting together a few rows back. April waved and Natalie Donovan gave her a thumbs-up sign. A little bit of the tension knotted in her chest eased.

A tap on her shoulder had her swinging back around.

"It's not Halloween," Miriam Thompson, Charles's wife, said in a disapproving hiss as she made her way into the seat next to Emily, with Aaron's brother, Todd, on her other side. Aaron wasn't with them, a fact for which Emily was grateful. "You should show some respect to the seriousness of this election."

Red-hot anger rushed through Emily. Anger at Miriam for making the comment, at Jase for asking her to do this but mostly at herself for still caring what people thought of her and her son. Before she could respond, her mother whipped around in her seat.

"You should shut your mouth, Miriam," Meg said. "Before I come over there and do it for you. My grandson can be a superhero every day if it makes him happy." She wagged a finger at each of the Thompsons. "We could use more heroes in this town, not people who feel like it's their right to taunt and bully others."

Miriam gasped but turned away, her cheeks coloring bright pink as she made her son shift seats so she wasn't sitting right beside Emily.

Emily tried to hide her shocked smile as she leaned over Davey toward her mother and spoke low. "'Come over there and do it for you'?"

Meg sniffed. "I never liked that woman."

A hush fell over the room as Liam Donovan walked onto the stage, along with Jase and Charles. Liam was moderating the meeting. A few general announcements were made first and then Liam formally introduced Jase and Charles, although Emily couldn't imagine there was anyone in the room who didn't know either man. Crimson had grown in the years since she'd been gone, but it seemed as though everyone in attendance tonight had some history with the town.

The thought made her encouraged for Jase, as so much of Crimson's recent boom could be attributed to work he'd done as part of the city council. No wonder he was torn between making decisions for his own happiness and his duty to the town.

Charles took the mic first, detailing his background as former sheriff. Emily gritted her teeth as he made special mention of his long marriage, and his family's history of service and philanthropy in Crimson.

Jase didn't seem bothered, though, and stepped to the podium after shaking Charles's hand. He smiled as he looked out over the audience.

"It's great to see so many friendly and familiar faces in this crowd," he began. "This town means a lot to me and no matter what our differences, we can all agree that we want the best and brightest future for Crimson." After a ripple of applause, he spoke again. "I'd like to personally thank Charles for his contributions to our town over the years. Families like the Thompsons gave us a strong foundation. As many of you know, my family's history runs in a different direction." He chuckled softly. "Which is why I'm especially grateful for this town and the people in it."

Emily didn't turn around but she could feel the energy building in the crowd as Jase spoke. He was sincere and articulate, not shying away from where he came from but taking the power of his family's troubled history away from Charles by owning it himself. She'd never been prouder. Then she felt Davey shift next to her. It was hard to tell whether he was reacting to the excitement of the crowd or Jase's voice booming through the room or one of any number of things that might disturb his equilibrium.

The reason didn't matter. Something was also building inside Davey. He fidgeted, tugging on the tights of his superhero costume and humming softly under his breath. She reached in her purse and grabbed the bag of Lego pieces.

"Here, sweetie," she said, placing them gently in his lap. Keeping her voice calm and trying to regulate her own energy was key for keeping him from moving any closer to a meltdown.

Her mom shot her a look but Emily shook her head. It didn't matter what anyone thought at the moment. She had to keep Davey calm or everything she'd worked so hard to create would blow up in her face.

Davey opened the bag and methodically pulled out building pieces.

Emily breathed a tentative sigh of relief and focused on Jase. He was looking directly at her.

"With me tonight," he said, "is a family who have

made me a part of their own over the years." His gaze left hers, but she could still feel the warmth of it across her skin. "What makes this town special is that we take care of each other. Meg and Jacob Crawford took care of me when I needed it most. As mayor, I want to make sure we continue to move Crimson forward and, more importantly, that we continue to look out for one another."

"I guess your own father isn't part of your grand plan?" The loud, slurring voice rang out in the quiet of the meeting room. Emily heard the crowd's collective gasp but kept her eyes on Jase. His expression registered shock, confusion and finally a resigned disappointment as he looked out past the audience toward the back of the room. His gaze flicked to hers for a moment. The silent plea in his chocolate-brown eyes registered deep in her heart even as he schooled his features into a carefully controlled mask once again.

"You count, Dad," he said calmly into the microphone. "But we should talk later."

Emily turned to the back of the room to see Declan making his way up the center aisle. The door to the hallway was swinging closed and she caught a glimpse of a figure moving to the side as it shut. Aaron Thompson.

She got up immediately and moved toward Jase's dad.

"Why the hell aren't I up there with your fake family?" Declan yelled. "I'm part of this town, too. Or have you forgotten why you wanted to become such a do-gooder in the first place, Jase?"

"Declan, don't do this," she said as she got closer. The smell of liquor coming off him hit her so hard she took a step back. She had to get him out of this meeting. "This isn't you talking." She tried to make her voice gentle. "It's the alcohol. Jase needs you to get it under control. Now."

His bloodshot eyes tracked to her. "Oh, yeah, sweetheart. My son loves control. He can't tolerate anything less than total perfection." He motioned a shaky finger between himself and Emily. "The two of us are bound to disappoint him."

The words struck a nerve but she smiled and reached for his hand. "Then let's get out of here."

She could see Sheriff Bennett moving around the edge of the room toward them. A glance over her shoulder showed Jase stepping out from behind the podium toward the edge of the stage. She shook her head, hoping to diffuse Declan's alcohol-filled rant before it had a chance to gather steam.

She took his arm just as she heard Davey cry out, "Mommy, my spaceship. It broke." Her son's voice was a keening cry. "It broke!"

"I won't be handled," Declan yelled and tore his hand away from her grasp.

But Emily's attention was on Davey so instead of letting go she stumbled forward, plowing into Declan's chest and sending them both into the edge of the chair at the end of the row.

Edna Sharpe occupied the chair, and as it tipped, the three of them tumbled to the floor. Emily saw stars as her head slammed into the chair.

All hell broke loose.

People from the nearby rows surrounded them. Edna screamed and flailed at the bottom of the pile. "My ankle. You broke my ankle."

Declan moaned. "I think I'm going to be sick."

Emily scrambled to get out from under him but his thigh was pinning her down.

"Mommy!" Davey screeched, his voice carrying over the din of noise to her. "I lost a piece to my spaceship."

She pushed at Declan, recognizing the mounting hysteria in Davey's tone. Cole Bennett was there a second later, but it was too late. Jase's father coughed, then threw up, the vile liquid hitting Emily's shoulder as she tried to turn away.

He was hauled off her then and she stood, the crowd surrounding them parting as she pushed her way through. One bonus to being puked on—it cleared a path quicker than anything else.

Jase was trying to shoulder his way down the aisle, yelling at people as he moved.

Davey had started shrieking now, and she knew a full-blown meltdown could last for several minutes to close to an hour. Meg met her gaze and whispered, "I'm sorry." Meg picked a screaming Davey up and carried him out the side door of the meeting room.

Emily shook her head as she followed. There was nothing her sweet mother could have done to prevent this moment. The responsibility was Emily's. And she failed. Miserably.

Jase was in front of her a second later. She expected understanding. Instead, he glared at her. "What the hell, Em? You tackled my dad. Is Edna really hurt? This is a mess."

She blinked, unable to process the accusation in his tone, let alone to respond. "I've got to get to Davey," she whispered.

His muffled screams echoed from the hall.

Jase ran a hand through his hair. "Can you get control of him? The screaming is only making this disaster worse."

She reeled back as if he'd slapped her. A disaster. That's how Jase saw her attempt at helping him. Her head was ringing from where she'd hit the corner of the chair. Her son was having a public meltdown. And she was covered in vomit.

"We've got to pull out of this," Jase said, searching her gaze as if he expected her to have a magic solution.

"I'm going to my son," she said, pushing at him. "He's not part of a disaster. He's a scared little boy who shouldn't have been put in this situation in the first place."

"The sheriff has your dad out the door," Liam called from where he stood on the stage. "I'm going to get everyone back to their seats."

Jase closed his eyes for a moment and his gaze was gentler when he opened them again. "I didn't mean it like that. Em…"

"No." She pushed away. It was too late. She knew better. Davey was all that mattered, her only priority. "I've got to get him out of here. Take care of your image or your dad. I don't care. I'm not your problem, Jase. We're not yours."

She hurried down the row, bending to pick up a stray Lego piece as she walked. She found Davey and her mother at the end of the hallway, Davey standing stiffly in front of the wooden bench where her mother sat. She crouched in front of him. "I have the missing piece," she said. He continued to scream, his eyes shut tight and his cheeks blotchy pink as he heaved breaths in and out between shrieks. "Davey, sweetie. Look at Mommy. I have the Lego piece. You can finish the spaceship."

His screaming subsided to an anxious whine as he looked at the small yellow brick she held in front of him. Emily held her breath. He hiccuped and reached for it, holding it gently between his first two fingers. "Thank you, Mommy." He wiped at his cheeks with the back of his sleeve. "Can we go home now? You're stinky."

She let out a ragged laugh. Or maybe it was a sob. Hard to tell with the emotions swirling inside her. "Yes, Wavy-Davey, we can go home now."

She straightened, meeting her mother's worried gaze. "I'm so sorry," Meg whispered.

Emily shook her head. "No kind words, Mom. I need to keep it together until we get back to the farm."

Meg's mouth thinned but she nodded. "You might want to take off the sweater."

Emily carefully pulled the nasty sweater over her head, gagging a little as the scent of vomit hit her again. It had been easy enough to ignore when adrenaline was fueling her. But now the reality of everything that had happened—in front of most of the town and everyone who mattered to her—made her want to curl up in a tiny ball. But she still had her son to take care of, which was the only thing keeping her going.

She stuffed the sweater into a nearby trash can. The memories of this horrible evening would prevent her from ever wearing it again.

"Let's go home," she said and her mother took her hand and led them toward the car.

Chapter Fourteen

Jase had returned to the stage after Emily left and Declan had been hauled away. He'd remained calm even though he'd wanted to walk to the front of that room and rip Charles Thompson to shreds. Everything he'd worked for had been destroyed, but he'd seen Aaron Thompson slip into the hallway as the door closed to the back of the meeting room. At that moment he realized how personal the Thompsons felt about his failure and what lengths they were willing to go to make sure he wasn't elected mayor.

None of that really mattered. All he cared about was the hurt in Emily's eyes as he'd demanded she quiet Davey. It had been his shame talking. She didn't deserve the pain he'd caused her. He'd wanted to follow her to the Crawfords' farm right away, but there had been so much fallout to deal with after the scene his dad had caused.

Jase publicly apologized for his dad's behavior. He wanted to call out Charles Thompson, but he wouldn't stoop to Thompson's level or make excuses for Declan. It had been even more difficult to keep his temper in check when Charles complained as Liam officially ended the meeting and sent the crowd home.

Several of Jase's friends had offered words of encouragement and support, but he could barely hear them over the roar in his head. Jake Travers deemed Edna's ankle only a sprain but she insisted on going to the hospital for an X-ray, so Jase stayed with her until her daughter arrived to take her home. Cole offered to let Declan ride out his bender in one of the town's holding cells.

Jase didn't bother to comment on the irony of his father in jail as he was trying to make a bid to lead the town. It was his worst nightmare come to life.

At least he'd thought it was until arriving at the ranch. Meg had come to the door before he'd knocked.

"I need to see her," he said and opened the screen.

Meg crossed her arms over her chest. "No, Jase."

"I only need a minute," he pleaded, letting the emotions he'd tried to tamp down spill into his tone. "I'll wait if she's putting Davey to bed. Maybe I could—"

"No." Meg's normally warm gaze was frigid as she met his. "She was trying to support you tonight even though it wasn't what she wanted. You hurt her when things went bad." She shook her head. "My daughter has been down that road before, and she's only begun to recover from the pain of it. I won't let her be treated that way again. She deserves better."

"I know." He felt desperate in a way he hadn't in years. He could feel the person he loved slipping away from him, only this time it was his own fault. "I let the moment get the best of me. I love her, Meg."

"You want her, Jase. You have for years. I get that, but it isn't the same as love. What happened tonight wasn't love."

"I made a mistake."

"You might not be the right man for her."

"You're wrong."

"I hope I am, and if Emily decides to allow you back into her life, I won't stop her. But for now she doesn't want to see you. You have enough to deal with in your own life. Focus on that."

"I don't care about anything else." The words came out louder than he'd intended and he forced himself to take a calming breath. "At least tell her I was here. Tell her I'm sorry. Please, Meg."

After a moment she nodded. "You're a good man, Jase. You don't have anything to prove to this town but it's time you start believing it." She backed up and shut the door, leaving him alone on the porch.

This house was the one place he'd always felt safe and welcome, and now he'd messed that up along with his relationship with Emily.

It was close to midnight by the time Jase walked into the sheriff's office. He would have been there earlier, but Cole had texted that his dad was sleeping and he'd alert Jase when Declan woke up. Jase had gone home after leaving the Crawfords' and let Ruby into the yard. As the puppy chased shadows around in the porch light, Jase had sat on the top step and left messages for each of the town council members to apologize for the spectacle his father had created at the meeting.

Declan was sitting on the bench in the holding cell when Jase walked into the office.

"It isn't locked," Cole told him, getting up from his chair, "but he said he wouldn't come out until you got here." He patted Jase on the arm. "I'm going to give the two of you some time. I'll be out front. Let me know if you need anything."

Jase walked forward, wrapped his fingers around the cool iron of the holding cell's bars. "You ready, Dad?"

Declan snorted. "That's all you've got to say to me?"

"If you're looking for me to apologize," Jase ground out, his temper sparking even through the numbness of his exhaustion, "forget it. Drying out in this cell was the safest place for you tonight. After the stunt you pulled—"

"You shouldn't be here." His dad stood, paced from one end of the small cell to the other. "You don't owe me anything, least of all an apology. Why the hell aren't you with Emily?"

"Let's go home."

"I puked on her."

"Yep."

Declan rubbed a hand over his face. "I'm sorry."

"Emily is the one who's owed an apology. Maybe she'll talk to you."

"She won't speak to you?"

Jase shook his head. "Come on, Dad. I'm tired and done with this day."

His father lowered himself back down to the metal bench. "You see me here."

"I see you," Jase said quietly, hating the memories the image conjured.

"This is *me* in here, Jase. Not you. I did this to myself, like my dad and his dad before him. Our trouble is not your responsibility."

"It sure as hell felt like it when you barged into the town hall meeting drunk out of your mind."

"I slipped," Declan said. "I let people get to me and I took one drink."

"One drink ended in the bottom of the bottle. I've seen it too many times, Dad. You can't stop at one drink."

"I know, and I didn't want to. I wanted to lose myself. To forget about everything for a little while."

"Aaron Thompson brought you to the meeting."

"It wasn't his fault, even as much as I'd like it to be. I was at the bar when he found me. Yeah," Declan admitted, "he said some things that set me off more."

"They wanted me to be humiliated."

"I brought tonight's shame on you, Jase. Not the Thompsons. I'm the reason you can't have a life of your own."

"I have a life," Jase argued, but his voice sounded flat to his own ears. Because without Emily he had nothing. "I thought we agreed the town hall meeting was too much for you. If I knew—"

"It wasn't the meeting." Declan stood, reached into the back pocket of his jeans and pulled out a small envelope. "Nearly twenty years later and she can still set me off." He handed the envelope to Jase. "It's a letter from your mom, son."

Jase stared at the loopy cursive on the front of the envelope, disbelief ripping through him. "Why didn't she track down my email or cell number? No one sends letters anymore."

"Your mother was always an original." Declan

moved toward the door to the cell. "I don't know what she wrote, but I hope whatever it is gives you some closure."

"Why after all this time?"

"I don't know." He stopped, cupped his rough hand around Jase's cheek. The smell of stale liquor seeped from his skin, both familiar and stomach churning. "What I hope she says is that leaving had nothing to do with you. That she regrets not taking you with her and giving you the life you deserve." His smile was sad as he ruffled Jase's hair. "That's what I hope she says, but I don't want to know. Bennett let me use the phone when I woke up. My AA sponsor is coming by the house in the morning. Whether you believe me or not, this was a one-time mistake."

Jase stood there staring at the envelope for a few more seconds, then turned. "Dad."

Declan turned back, his handle on the door to the outer office. "Yeah?"

"I don't regret staying with you."

"Are you sure you won't stay with Mom?" Noah pulled out from the farm's driveway and started toward town. He and Katie had been home from their honeymoon for a few days so Emily had asked him to go apartment hunting with her.

"I can't keep hiding out there." Emily read the address to the first building, which was in a new development on the far side of town. She watched the midday sun bounce off the snow-dusted peak at the top of Crimson Mountain. The weather was cooler now, and while there hadn't been any snow yet in town, winter would be closing in soon.

"That's not how she thinks of it."

"Doesn't make it less true." She shifted to look at her brother, still tan from his honeymoon on the beach. "I'm staying in Crimson, Noah. I need to start making a life for Davey and me."

"He still likes school?"

She smiled. "He loves it. Since I'm now working in the elementary school front office, I can check in on him during the day." The kindergarten teacher, Erin Mac-Donald, had made a visit to the farm when Emily kept Davey home from school the day after his public melt-down. While Davey had spent the day building Lego sets and baking cupcakes with his grandma, Emily'd barely been able to get out of bed.

The teacher's sensitivity to Davey's outburst had made its way through Emily's fragile defenses and she'd broken down with all the details of her messed-up life. Erin had immediately called the school principal. The new secretary he'd hired had quit after only two weeks. Emily had an interview the following afternoon and started work the next day. "Millie Travers told me Ms. MacDonald was a great teacher, but she's more. She's a great person." She nudged her brother. "Turns out Crimson is full of great people. Davey is getting access to the resources he needs. He's made a friend—"

"In addition to Brooke?"

"Brooke is his *best* friend," Emily clarified. "But, yes, another boy who loves Lego building. They mainly play side by side, but it's a start."

"Does Henry know how he's doing?"

"I sent him an email," Emily admitted with a shrug. "I don't know what I was hoping for, but he's Davey's father so I thought…" She sighed. "His assistant responded to it."

"The guy is a total idiot."

"Agreed. But we're doing okay without him."

Noah turned onto the road that led into town. The aspen leaves were turning brilliant yellow, shimmering in the sunlight. It gave Emily a bright and shiny glow inside her.

"What about the other idiot in your life?" Noah glanced over at her.

"Jase isn't in my life." She paused, then whispered, "and he's not an idiot."

"You haven't talked to him?"

"You know I haven't, Noah." She'd asked April to go to his office the morning after the meeting to give him Emily's resignation letter. Maybe she should have been brave enough to face him, but the humiliation she'd felt after that night had been too raw.

"Why?"

"There's nothing to say. We want different things." She kept waiting for the pain to ease, the vise around her heart to release. Every time she thought of Jase, her whole body reverberated with the deep ache of missing him. "I hear the election is going well." She'd tried not to hear, not to listen but it was difficult in a small town where people were happy to pass around gossip like it was breaking news.

Noah nodded. "Hard to believe the stunt his dad pulled at the town hall meeting actually helped him in the campaign."

"Not hard with Jase."

"Everyone is talking about how much he's overcome and how he's a self-made success."

"He deserves every bit of his success," Emily said quietly. The Thompsons' plan to discredit Jase in the eyes of voters had backfired. She wasn't the only one who'd seen Aaron as he sent Declan into the town hall meeting. Apparently, Charles had a reputation of bending the rules while he'd been sheriff and no one wanted a man with a twisted moral compass in charge of the town.

"You missed the turn." She straightened in her seat as Noah took a right toward Crimson High School.

"I have a quick stop to make."

"What stop?"

He pulled over to the curb at the edge of the football field. "I'll show you. Hop out."

There were a few teenagers throwing a ball on the field but the stands were empty.

"Do you see it?"

She climbed out of the truck, scanning the bleachers for something familiar. "See what, Noah?"

The truck's engine roared to life and she whirled around. Noah had rolled down the passenger window. "See me making you really angry."

"Have you lost your mind?"

He grimaced. "According to my new wife. I hope you'll forgive me, and I'll be back in ten minutes."

"What are you talking about?"

Noah blew her a kiss and drove off, leaving Emily standing on the sidewalk. She didn't even have her phone. "I'm going to kill him," she muttered.

"It's not his fault," a voice said behind her. She went stock-still even as her knees threatened to sag. "He owed me for something and I called in the favor. He didn't have a choice."

She turned to face Jase, letting anger rise to the top of the mountain of emotions vying for space in her heart. "Of course he had a choice," she said on a hiss of breath. "The same way I have a choice as to which one of you I'm going to murder first."

He took a step toward her and she backed up. "Don't come any closer."

"We need to talk."

She shook her head. What she needed was to get the hell out of there before she gave in to the temptation to plaster herself against him. "No. We don't."

"I need to talk," he clarified.

"Talk to someone who wants to listen to what you have to say."

He ran his hands through his hair, looking as miserable as she felt. "Don't you understand? I only ever cared about you. From the start, Emily."

She closed her eyes and stuck her fingers in her ears, repeating the words *I can't hear you* in a singsong voice.

His hands were on her arms a moment later. She flinched away but secretly wanted to melt into him. She'd missed his warmth. Missed the scent of him, pine and soap and man. Missed everything about him.

"Open your eyes," he said, his tone an irresistible mix of amusement and desperation.

She did, keeping her gaze trained on the football field. Davey would like the symmetry of the lines dissecting the green grass.

"This was where I fell in love with you the first time," Jase whispered, following her gaze. "Every weekend you were at the football games, surrounded by a group of friends. You took great pleasure in ignoring me."

"You were my older brother's best friend. I had no use for you." She glanced back at him and her heart skipped a beat. He was watching her as if it was the first time he'd seen her. As if she really was the only thing he cared about in life.

"And still I was ruined for any other girl." His fingers brushed her hair away from her face. "I remember you on those cool fall nights, bundled up in sweaters and boots, your blond hair like a calling card as you held court in the bleachers. You were the most perfect girl I'd ever seen."

She took a step back, out of his grasp and tried to get a handle on her emotions. "I was a brat."

"I didn't care." His chocolate-brown gaze never wavered as he spoke.

"Why are you telling me this now?"

"Because you need to understand it was always you, Em. You were the first and only thing I ever wanted." He flashed a wry smile and toed his boot against the gravel. "Back then it was because you embodied the perfection that was never a part of my life."

"I wasn't perfect and—"

He pressed his finger to her lips. "Then you returned and *I* got a chance to make you happy. No, you're not perfect. Neither am I. But *real* is better than perfect." He scrubbed a hand over his face and the scratch of his stubble made her melt. Just a little. "I messed up, and I'm sorry. Sorrier than you'll ever know. I let the shame I felt about my own family change me."

"I understand."

"How can you understand when I don't?" He shook his head. "There's no excuse, Emily. I love that boy. Hell, I found myself putting together a Lego town the

other night with the bin of blocks you left at the house.
I miss him. I miss you."

"I understand life is messy. I wanted it to be put in
easy compartments. Even Davey, especially Davey."

"You came here to protect him. I get it."

She shook her head. "I came here to hide. Henry
wasn't the only one who failed him. Mothers have
dreams for their kids. To-the-moon whoppers like,
Will he grow up to be President? And the dreams that
really mattered. *Will he have friends? Will he be happy?*
I felt like I lost control of those the first time I noticed
Davey's differences."

He stared at her, patiently waiting as always.

"I want to live life celebrating who he is."

Just when she thought it couldn't get any more painful, Jase ripped open another layer of her heart. "I want
that, too, Em. I love you both so much."

And another layer. "I'm pulling out of the mayor's
race."

"No," she whispered. "You wouldn't."

"I have a meeting with the council later this afternoon to officially withdraw my name."

"But you're going to win. Charles Thompson—"

"The reasons Charles is running for mayor are as
convoluted as mine." The half smile he gave her was
weary and strained. A different type of heartache roared
through her knowing his distress was her fault. Jase
had helped her regain her confidence and spirit, and
she'd repaid him by allowing her fears to bring both
of them low.

"Your reasons aren't convoluted." She moved to him
then, put a hand on his arm. "You are straightforward
and selfless. You've done so much already—"

"Trust me, I know what it's like to have fear rule your life. No matter how much I do, I'm scared it isn't enough to make amends for all the mistakes. I worry I'll never be enough."

"Those mistakes weren't yours, but the choice to make a different future for yourself has been." He was standing before her, willing to give up everything he'd built in this town. His whole life. The searing thought that this was exactly what her ex-husband had expected of her almost brought her to her knees.

"My mother contacted me," he said softly. "Her letter is what made Dad drink again."

"Oh, Jase."

He ran a hand through his hair, his jaw tight. "She's sick, and she wants to see me. After so many years, she apologized for leaving."

"You deserve that."

He trailed his fingers over hers, his touch sending shivers of awareness across her skin. "I want to deserve you, Em. We deserve happiness. Together. Give me another chance to prove how much you mean to me. How much I love you."

She pressed a hand to her chest as if she could quell the pounding of her heart. He was willing to give her exactly what she'd wanted from Henry, but it was so wrong. She loved him for his dedication and sense of duty, for the very *rightness* of who he was. She couldn't allow loving her to destroy his dream. "You can't give up the campaign, Jase."

"I will if it means a chance with you."

"It isn't… You don't…" She took a breath, trying to give her words time to catch up with her racing thoughts. "I wanted to make my life manageable again, but love isn't manageable and neither is everything that comes with it. Life is messy. If I hide from the pain, I risk never having the love. So I'm going to stop hiding. I love Davey the way he is—"

"Me, too," he whispered, his voice raw.

"I know." She reached up, cupped his face with her hands. "You must know you're already enough for the people in this town. For me. You're the one who has to believe it now. I want to support you, even when it's a struggle. We'll find a way. I may not be the perfect politician's wife but—"

"I don't want you to be perfect. I want you, all of you. Your bossiness and your skyscraper-tall defensive walls—"

"Hey." She poked him in the chest.

"I want the way you love Davey so fiercely, the way you bullied me into stepping into my own life." He lifted a hand to trail it across her jaw. "I want you when you're fragile and vulnerable, when you're strong and stubborn. I want Davey and a house full of Lego creations." He dipped his head so they were at eye level. "I want you every day for the rest of our lives."

"You're going to win this election, Jase." She felt tears slip down her cheeks. "You are the best thing I never expected to happen in my life." She wrapped her arms around his neck and brushed her lips across his. "How did I miss seeing you for so long?"

"The only thing that matters is we're here now." He lifted her into his embrace. "Tell me you'll give us another chance."

She laughed. "A thousand chances, Jase. Because if you take me on, it's going to be for good."

"For good and forever," he agreed. "Be mine forever."

"Yes," she whispered. "Forever."

He took over the kiss, making it at once tender and fully possessive. Emily lost herself in the moment, in the feel of him and the happiness bubbling up inside her like a newly unearthed spring.

A honking horn had her jerking away a moment later.

"Get a room," Noah called as he slowed the truck. He grinned at her. "I hope this means you're not mad at me."

"I'm not mad," she called. "But you're still in trouble."

His gaze flicked to Jase. "Are you going to help me with her?"

Emily growled as Jase laughed. "I wouldn't be dumb enough to try."

Emily patted him on the shoulder. "Which is why you get a thousand chances." She pointed at her brother. "You get none."

He blew her a kiss and she couldn't stop her smile.

"Are we still going apartment hunting?" Noah asked.

"She's got a home," Jase answered. "With me."

"And I get to pick the paint colors?" Emily asked, raising a brow.

"You get to do whatever you want."

She kissed him again. "What I want is to spend the rest of my life with you." She felt color rise to her cheeks, realizing she'd said too much too soon.

Jase only smiled. "I've only been waiting most of my life," he said, dropping to one knee and pulling a small velvet box out of his jacket pocket. "Emily, will you marry me?"

She swallowed, struggled to take a breath and nodded. He slipped the ring on her finger and stood to take her in his arms once more.

"Katie is going to be so mad she missed this moment," she heard her brother yell. "Good thing I got the whole event on video. Congratulations, you two crazy kids." Noah honked once more, then drove out of the parking lot.

"I love you, Em," Jase whispered. "Forever."

"Forever," she repeated and felt her heart fill with all the happiness it could carry.

* * * * *

Look for
CHRISTMAS ON CRIMSON MOUNTAIN,
the next book in Michelle Major's
CRIMSON, COLORADO *miniseries*
coming in December 2016

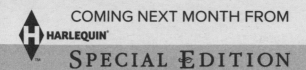

COMING NEXT MONTH FROM

HARLEQUIN®

SPECIAL EDITION

Available August 23, 2016

#2497 A MAVERICK AND A HALF
Montana Mavericks: The Baby Bonanza • by Marie Ferrarella
Anderson Dalton is suddenly a daddy—to a ten-year-old! Romance is the last thing
on his mind, but love finds him in the form of Marina Laramie, a schoolteacher with
a bouncing baby of her own. Marina offers a marriage of convenience, just for the
kids' sake, of course. But when long-kept secrets come out, will their fake marriage
have a chance to become the real deal?

#2498 A CAMDEN'S BABY SECRET
The Camdens of Colorado • by Victoria Pade
Widowed Livi Camden had only ever kissed her late husband and is sure he was
her only chance at love and happiness. At least until one wild night on a Hawaiian
business trip leaves her pregnant with former bad boy Callan Tierney's baby.
Will career-minded Callan and still-grieving Livi be able to give their new family a
chance?

#2499 HER TEXAS RESCUE DOCTOR
Texas Rescue • by Caro Carson
Grace Jackson has been the unassuming, overworked personal assistant to a
Hollywood movie star all her life—after all, the movie star is her big sister. To save
her sister's career from bad publicity, Grace turns a quiet geek of an emergency
room doctor, Alex Gregory, into the perfect escort for a celebrity-studded charity
ball. But has she created the perfect man for her sister...or for herself?

#2500 A WORD WITH THE BACHELOR
The Bachelors of Blackwater Lake • by Teresa Southwick
Erin Riley has a new gig as a book coach with bestselling author Jack Garner. He
may be a monosyllabic grump, but she's never been this drawn to a client. Jack is
beginning to believe he is a one-hit wonder and doesn't want to be pulled into her
sunny disposition. These two might have opposite personalities, but maybe that's
what will help them heal their equally battered hearts.

#2501 MEET ME AT THE CHAPEL
The Brands of Montana • by Joanna Sims
Rancher Brock McCallister hasn't found much to laugh about recently, but when
eternal optimist Casey Brand moves into the apartment above the barn, she brings
much-needed light into his autistic daughter's life...and his own. When tragedy
strikes, he must convince Casey that the three of them can be the family she's
always wanted and the second chance at love he deserves.

#2502 THE COWGIRL'S FOREVER FAMILY
The Cedar River Cowboys • by Helen Lacey
The last thing Brooke Laughton expected to see when she opened her door was
sexy lawyer Tyler Madden with a baby in his arms. Turns out, she has a niece! While
they wait for her brother to return and claim the baby, Brooke and Tyler give in to a
deep attraction, but old fears threaten to keep them apart.

**YOU CAN FIND MORE INFORMATION ON UPCOMING HARLEQUIN® TITLES,
FREE EXCERPTS AND MORE AT WWW.HARLEQUIN.COM.**

HSECNM0816

A makeover, a doctor, a movie star.
It should be the beginning of a red-carpet romance,
but Dr. Alex Gregory is more interested in the
unassuming assistant, Grace Jackson,
who just happens to be the movie star's sister.

Read on for a sneak preview of
HER TEXAS RESCUE DOCTOR,
the new book in Caro Carson's
***TEXAS RESCUE** miniseries.*

Alex didn't wait for a request to stand next to Grace. He walked up to her, tuning out the cluster of people who'd invaded his house. "You look very, very beautiful."

"Thank you."

Princess Picasso gave an order. "You two should dance. I need to see if I'll be able to move in it. What kind of music are they going to be playing, anyway?"

Grace didn't look away, so neither did he, but she answered her sister. "Some country-and-western bands. Pretty big names. We have a dance lesson scheduled later today."

"I know how to waltz and two-step." Alex stepped closer and picked up her hand. "Do you?"

"I waltz." They assumed the traditional position of a man and a woman in a ballroom dance, and Alex took the first step.

Grace's voice was as lovely as everything else about her. She counted to three over and over in a little nonsense melody, smiling at him, his beautiful golden girl, silver in his arms, glowing with happiness.

He realized he was smiling back.

So this is happiness. He recognized it, although it had been a very long time since he'd felt it. It was not equilibrium. There was no balance. He was absolutely at the far end of a scale, a feeling of pure pleasure unadulterated by pain—yet.

There was always pain. He knew that, but at this moment, he couldn't imagine ever feeling pain again, not with Grace in his arms.

"One, two, three. One, two, three."

"You look wonderful," the stylist said, clapping. "Sophia, what do you think?"

He and Grace had to stop, or risk looking like fools. She gave his hand a friendly squeeze as she stepped out of his arms. A *friendly* squeeze. Friends. There was pain in being friends with someone he desired so keenly.

Don't miss
HER TEXAS RESCUE DOCTOR by Caro Carson,
available September 2016 wherever
Harlequin® Special Edition books and ebooks are sold.

www.Harlequin.com

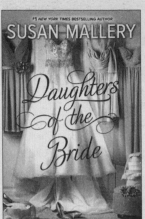

THE WORLD IS BETTER WITH

Romance

Harlequin has everything from contemporary, passionate and heartwarming to suspenseful and inspirational stories.

Whatever your mood,
we have a romance just for you!

Connect with us to find your next great read, special offers and more.

f /HarlequinBooks

🐦 @HarlequinBooks

www.HarlequinBlog.com

www.Harlequin.com/Newsletters

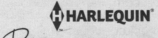

⟨H⟩ HARLEQUIN®

A *Romance* FOR EVERY MOOD™

www.Harlequin.com

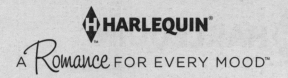

HARLEQUIN®

A *Romance* FOR EVERY MOOD™

JUST CAN'T GET ENOUGH?

Join our social communities
and talk to us online.

You will have access to the latest
news on upcoming titles and special
promotions, but most importantly,
you can talk to other fans about your
favorite Harlequin reads.

Harlequin.com/Community

Facebook.com/HarlequinBooks

Twitter.com/HarlequinBooks

Pinterest.com/HarlequinBooks

Love the Harlequin book you just read?

Your opinion matters.

Review this book on your favorite book site, review site, blog or your own social media properties and share your opinion with other readers!

Be sure to connect with us at:
Harlequin.com/Newsletters
Facebook.com/HarlequinBooks
Twitter.com/HarlequinBooks